KIKI'S
DELIVERY SERVICE

KIKI'S DELIVERY SERVICE

EIKO KADONO

TRANSLATED BY
EMILY BALISTRIERI

ILLUSTRATIONS BY
YUTA ONODA

DELACORTE PRESS

Translation copyright © 2020 by Penguin Random House LLC
Jacket art and interior illustrations copyright © 2020 by Yuta Onoda

All rights reserved. Published in the United States by Delacorte Press, an imprint
of Random House Children's Books, a division of Penguin Random House LLC,
New York. Originally published in Japan and in paperback under the title *Majyo no
Takkyubin* by Fukuinkan Shoten Publishers, Inc., Tokyo, in 1985. Text copyright
© 1985 by Eiko Kadono. The English rights arranged with Fukuinkan Shoten
Publishers, Inc., Tokyo through The English Agency (Japan) Ltd. All rights reserved.

Delacorte Press is a registered trademark and the colophon
is a trademark of Penguin Random House LLC.

Visit us on the Web! rhcbooks.com

Educators and librarians, for a variety of teaching tools, visit us at
RHTeachersLibrarians.com

Library of Congress Cataloging-in-Publication Data
Names: Kadono, Eiko, author. | Onoda, Yuta, illustrator. |
Balistrieri, Emily, translator.
Title: Kiki's delivery service / Eiko Kadono ; translated by Emily Balistrieri ;
illustrated by Yuta Onoda.
Description: First edition. | New York : Delacorte Press, [2020] | Audience:
Ages 8–12. | Audience: Grades 4–6. | Summary: "Thirteen-year-old half-witch
Kiki travels to the town of Koriko where she makes new friends,
overcomes challenges, and shares her magic with her community to
make the world a brighter place"— Provided by publisher.
Identifiers: LCCN 2019042296 (print) | LCCN 2019042297 (ebook) |
ISBN 978-1-9848-9666-7 (hardcover) | ISBN 978-1-9848-9668-1 (glb) |
ISBN 978-1-9848-9667-4 (ebook)
Subjects: CYAC: Witches—Fiction. | Delivery of goods—Fiction. |
Flight—Fiction. | Cats—Fiction.
Classification: LCC PZ7.K1167 Ki 2020 (print) |
LCC PZ7.K1167 (ebook) | DDC [E—dc23]

The text of this book is set in 10.5-point Chaparral Pro.
Interior design by Jen Valero

Printed in the United States of America
10 9 8 7 6 5 4 3 2 1
First Delacorte Press Edition

KIKI'S
DELIVERY SERVICE

THE SECRET OF THE MAGIC
A NOTE FROM THE AUTHOR

Kiki's Delivery Service was inspired by one of my daughter's drawings. It was a picture of a witch flying through the sky, listening to a radio. Musical notes danced around her. It reminded me of photos of New York City from a bird's-eye view that I'd seen in *Life,* an American magazine. They were beautiful images, and I felt there was a story there. If I wrote about a witch like the one my daughter drew, I could see the world through the eyes of a bird. I knew I would fly as an author, because writing fiction made me feel as though I had wings. I chose to make the protagonist witch a twelve-year-old, just like my daughter at the time. That's how *Kiki's Delivery Service* got its start.

I decided one thing right from the beginning: Kiki's

sole power would be flying through the sky on her broom. With only one type of magic, Kiki would need to use her brain to solve problems. Overcoming conflicts would help her grow, add some ups and downs to the story, and make her journey more interesting.

Kiki's magic is as close to normal as possible—it's everyday magic. She is a witch, but she's also a perfectly ordinary girl. She has the same worries, disappointments, and joys as anyone else, so I knew readers around her age would relate to her. And as I continued writing Kiki's story, I realized that even if you can't fly through the air like Kiki, you have your own unique power that is equally important.

As I wrote and revised, wrote and revised, I discovered that I loved writing. As long as I created stories, I could live an exciting life with new discoveries every day. And I decided that, if nothing else, I would continue writing as long as I live. I'll never forget the peace of mind I felt at that moment—I sensed the magic inside myself. I've come to believe that everyone has some type of magic inside them. If a person can find their magic and lovingly cultivate it, they'll truly feel alive every day.

There is magic inside each and every one of you, too—I believe that.

Now everyone in the United States can read Kiki's story. As the author, there is nothing that could make me happier.

Get ready, as Kiki is prepared to fly from Japan and deliver her story to you.

THE BEGINNING
OF THE STORY

Once, there was a little town sandwiched between a deep forest and gentle grassy hills. The town was built on an easy southward slope, its roofs the color of dark slices of toast all in a row. Clustered in the center of town, near the train station, were the town hall, the police station, the fire station, and the school. It was a normal town, one you could find anywhere.

But if you paid close attention, you'd find things you wouldn't usually see.

For instance, silver bells hung from the tops of tall trees. Even when it wasn't storming, these bells sometimes made a racket with their ringing. Then the townspeople would turn to each other and smile, saying, "Little Kiki must have gotten caught again."

But how could someone so "little" ring the bells in the treetops? Well, if you looked to the east and peeked into Kiki's home, you'd find the answer.

On a gate pillar facing the road hung a sign that read SNEEZE MEDICINE, right next to a big green gate that sat wide open. Beyond the gate was a large garden, and a single-story house. The garden grew herbs in neat rows with broad leaves and pointy leaves—all different kinds—and a pungent scent filled the area. The smell continued into the house and was strongest around the copper pot in the kitchen. From there you'd have a perfect view of the front living room wall. Instead of paintings or family photographs as you'd expect, two brooms made of bundled branches hung there, a big one and a little one. And from the living room you could hear the family's voices as they gathered for tea.

"Kiki, when are you planning to leave?" said a woman's voice, full of disapproval. "I think it's about time you let us know. You can't keep putting it off like this."

"That again?" A girl spoke now, somewhat annoyed. "Don't worry, Mom. I'm your daughter, after all. I *am* a witch. I'm thinking about it."

"How about leaving it up to Kiki, dear," a calm man interjected. "Until she decides for herself, you can prod all you want, but it won't make a difference."

"Yes, you might be right." The woman's voice rose slightly. "I'm just anxious. I feel responsible, you know?"

In this house lived a family of witches. Well, Kokiri, the mother, came from a long line of witches, and Okino, the father, was human. As a folklorist, he studied legends and tales about spirits and magic. Kiki was their only child, soon to turn thirteen.

The three were talking over tea about Kiki's coming-of-age day. When daughters of witches and humans reached the age of ten, they decided whether to follow tradition and live as witches themselves. If a girl picked this path, she promptly learned her mother's magic and chose a full-moon night of her thirteenth year as her coming-of-age day. For a young witch, this meant leaving her parents' house and moving to live on her own in a town or village in need of magic. Of course, finding a witchless town on her own is a difficult thing for a little girl to do. But over the years, witches' powers had grown weaker and their numbers had dropped. Such important tradition helped them survive, as well as share the existence of witches with as many towns, villages, and people as possible.

At age ten, Kiki had decided to become a witch and learn Kokiri's magic right away. Kokiri had two magic abilities. The first was growing herbs to make sneeze medicine, and the second was flying through the sky on a broom.

Kiki quickly got the hang of flying. But as she grew older, she often found herself distracted by all sorts of things—for example, the big pimples that started appearing on the sides of her nose, or deciding which dress she should wear to her friend's birthday party.

Whenever that happened, her broom would suddenly start to fall. One time she was so busy thinking about the scratchy new underwear she was wearing that she ran into a power line! Her broom broke into pieces, and Kiki herself ended up with bumps on her nose and both kneecaps.

Soon after, Kokiri tied bells to the tall trees of the forest. If Kiki was lost in thought and flying too low, her feet would ring the bells and the sound would bring her back to reality. Fortunately, they were ringing much less than they used to.

Meanwhile there was the sneeze-medicine-making, but Kiki didn't seem to be cut out for it. She was impatient and found it difficult to grow the herbs, finely chop the leaves and roots, and slowly simmer them.

"Will another type of magic disappear?" Kokiri lamented. In the olden days, witches could use all sorts of magic. But over the years, one type after another disappeared, until even a genuine witch like Kokiri was left with only two abilities. Now her daughter hated one of them, so it was no wonder she was upset.

"But it feels so much better to fly through the sky than stir a pot." Kiki didn't see what the issue was.

At these times, Okino would try to cheer Kokiri up. "Well, we can't force it. Maybe someday lost magic will be relearned. Plus, she has her black cat, doesn't she?"

Witches have long been accompanied by black cats. One could say that's another type of magic, too. When a witch has a baby girl, she searches for a black cat born around the same time and raises them together. As they grow, the cat and the girl learn to speak to each other in their own language. Kokiri used to have a cat named Mémé, and Kiki had one as well—a little black cat named Jiji. By the time the girl came of age, the cat would be a precious companion, and someone to turn to during good times and bad. Eventually the girl would grow up and find a new companion to take the place of her cat. The cat would also find its own partner and from then on, the pair would live separately.

KIKI COMES OF AGE

After tea, Kokiri and Okino went out to run errands while Kiki and Jiji sat dreamily at the garden's edge.

"I guess I should leave soon," Kiki said.

"You should. You're not going to decide you don't want to be a witch this late in the game, are you?" Jiji asked, looking up at her.

"Oh, of course not." Then the memory and thrill of her first time flying on a broom came rushing back.

For most of her life, Kiki was brought up more or less like any normal girl. She knew that her mother was a witch and that she would have to decide for herself one day whether she wanted to be one, too. Still, she never gave the decision serious thought. But a little while after she turned ten, she heard a friend of hers say, "I'm going to follow in my mom's footsteps and become a hairdresser." Kiki had a vague sense that Kokiri wanted her to follow in her footsteps, but she didn't wish to become a witch simply because of her mother.

I'm going to be whatever I want, Kiki thought. *I'm going to decide for myself.*

One day, Kokiri fashioned her daughter a little broom and asked, "Want to try flying?"

"Me? I can fly?"

"You're the daughter of a witch, so I should think so."

She could tell her mother was trying to lure her into taking up the family tradition, but it was a rare chance, so she agreed to learn the basics. Following Kokiri, she shyly mounted her broom and kicked off the ground.

Instantly, her body grew light—she was floating!

"I'm flying!" she shouted in spite of herself.

She was only about ten feet above the rooftop, but it felt incredible. The sky even seemed a little bluer. And on top of that, a curiosity welled up inside her, lifting both her heart and body. *I want to go higher—higher and higher. I wonder what I'll be able to see. What's it like up there? I need to know more.*

It was love at first flight. So of course she decided to become a witch.

"It's in your blood," Kokiri said with delight, but Kiki told herself, *No, it's not just that. I decided for myself.*

Suddenly Kiki jumped up from the grass. "Hey, Jiji, let's go check on my project. Just for a minute since Mom isn't here." She jerked her chin toward the shed in the corner of the garden.

"Why are you keeping it a secret from Kokiri, anyway?" Jiji moaned.

"'Cause she makes such a big deal out of anything to do with coming of age. And she always has to have her say, which makes everything more complicated than it needs to be."

"Well, I understand that. Anyhow, you need to make sure it gets lots of sun so it can properly dry out."

"Only a little."

"Okay, but don't bring it to bed again. If you sleep with it, it'll get moldy like last time."

"I know, I know. I need you to help me out, though. Pretty soon it'll be just us two."

As she spoke, she waded deftly through the waist-high herbs and angled her body into the space between the shed and the fence. Then she let out a happy yelp. "Look!"

A long, thin broom hung from the eaves of the shed. It gleamed in the westering sun.

"If it's this beautiful, I think it'll be okay," she squealed.

"Yeah, it seems like the drying process went well this time." Jiji looked up at her, wide-eyed. "Hey, Kiki, why don't you try flying? The weather's nice."

"I can't do that." Kiki shook her head. "I'm not using it until the day I leave. It'll be here soon. I want everything to be brand-new—my clothes, my shoes, and my broom, too. I want to be reborn. I'm sure Mom'll say, 'You're from a long line of witches, so you need to value the old.' But I'm me. I'm a new witch."

"So how am I supposed to make myself new?" Jiji pouted, his whiskers bristling.

"You're fine. I'll brush your fur till it shines. You'll be all fresh."

"Hmph." Jiji sniffed. "Fresh cat? Don't talk about it like you're going to cook me. You're not the only one coming of age, you know."

"You're right. I'm sorry." Kiki held back a laugh and looked into Jiji's eyes. "I wonder how it will feel to leave."

"I bet you'll cry."

"Ugh, no I won't."

"By the way, when are you finally planning to do it?" Jiji looked up at her again.

"Seems like we're ready, so we can leave pretty much any time. Want to make it the next night with a full moon?"

"What? The next one?"

"Yeah, in five more days. Doesn't it feel good to do something right when you decide?"

"This is going to be so much drama, as usual."

"I'll tell Mom and Dad tonight. I wonder what kind of town we'll end up in, Jiji." Kiki looked into the distance with a new, grown-up gleam in her eye.

"I don't know. I'm a bit worried, to be honest— since you're so quick with your decisions."

"Oh, I'm not worried at all. We can worry about things once they happen. Right now, I'm excited. It's like opening a present," she said breathlessly, and poked the broom. It swung back and forth as if it were nodding to her.

After dinner that evening, Kiki stood with Jiji before Kokiri and Okino. "You don't need to worry. I've decided when I'm going."

Kokiri leaped out of her chair. "Well! Really? When will it be?"

"The next night with a full moon."

Kokiri ran her eyes over the calendar on the wall, bewildered. "What? But that's only five days away. You should wait until the next one."

Kiki frowned and scrunched her shoulders. "See, there you go again! You get mad if I dillydally, but then you complain when I actually decide."

"She's right, dear. It's not quite fair," said Okino.

"Sure, but there's so much to get ready. It's a lot of work for a mother, too!" Flustered, Kokiri turned red.

Kiki leaned in to her face, shook her hips, and sang, "Believe in your daughter! Believe! I'm already ready. Right, Jiji?"

He twitched his tail in reply.

"What?" Kokiri's jaw dropped, and she lowered her eyes. "What do you mean, you're ready? What did you do?"

"I made a new broom. Jiji helped. Hold on, I'll go get it." Kiki opened the door and raced outside.

"Here it is!" She was back in no time, showing

Kokiri and Okino the broom she'd hidden by the shed.

"Oh, nicely done." Okino smiled.

"I soaked willow branches in the river and then left them in the sun. I did a good job, right, Mom?" Kiki swung the broom to show it off.

Kokiri slowly shook her head. "It's a beautiful broom, but you can't use it."

"Why not? I don't want to use that little broom I've had until now. Flying is the only magic thing I can do, so I at least want to fly on a nice new broom."

"If flying is the only magic thing you can do, doesn't that make your broom that much more important? What will you do if you have trouble flying on something you've never ridden before? Your start is critical. Coming of age isn't so easy." Kokiri shook her head again and continued. "We can only give you a little money, enough to eat for a year if you really keep your expenses down. After that, a witch has to survive on her magic. During this year, you need to figure out how to make a living—like how I prove myself useful to the townspeople by making medicine. Go with my broom. It's broken in, and you already know how to fly with it."

"Aw, I don't want to. It's all dirty and black, like

it's been used to clean a chimney! And the handle is so thick and heavy. It's clunky. Don't you think, Jiji?"

Jiji watched from near her feet and let out an exaggerated purr.

"See, Jiji agrees with me. He says a black cat riding that broom will get mistaken for a rain cloud, but on a willow broom, he'll look like a prince in a glass carriage."

"I don't know what to do with the two of you!" Kokiri exclaimed. "You're still a child, aren't you? Brooms aren't toys, you know. At some point my broom will get too old, and then you can use whatever you like. By then I'm sure you'll be a full-fledged witch." Kokiri suddenly closed her eyes, as if she was trying to think of something.

Kiki pouted and tapped the broom on the floor. "But what about the broom I made?"

"I'll use it instead. No problem with that, is there?"

Kiki glanced at her broom for a few moments, but then looked up and said, "Fine. But let me pick my dress. I saw a pretty one in a shop on Main Street— with a floral pattern! If I wear that, I'll look like a flying flower!"

"I'm sorry, but you can't do that, either." Kokiri had a serious expression on her face again. "These days, witches don't have to wear a pointy hat and a long cape, but the color of our clothes has always been the blackest black. That can't be changed."

That made Kiki sulk even more. "It's so old-fashioned. A black witch with a black cat—black, black, black."

"Well, of course it's old-fashioned. We come from old witch blood. Besides, black never goes out of style. Leave it to me. I'll make one in a hurry."

"This 'old blood' thing again . . . ," Kiki mumbled, pouting.

"Kiki, don't get too hung up on appearances. It's your heart that's important."

"Mom, I know that. I'll handle my heart. No one can *see* that, though." Kiki turned her resigned face to Okino. "Dad, you'll give me a radio, won't you? I want to listen to music while I fly. I'd really like a red radio."

"All right, all right. Got it." He nodded with a smile.

Kokiri smiled, then abruptly turned to her daughter. "Okay, that's enough for tonight. Good night, Kiki." And with her right hand, she used the hem of her apron to dab her eyes.

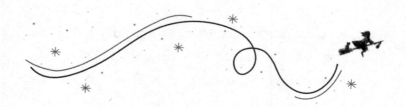

KIKI LANDS IN A BIG CITY

Every evening, the moon grew bigger and bigger, until the night it was finally full. Kiki's coming-of-age day had arrived.

That evening, when the sun started sinking in the west, Kiki put on the black dress her mother had made for her. She turned this way and that in the mirror, making it a whole production. Jiji, by her feet, wasn't about to be left out. He peeked into the mirror from the side, then stretched and curled his body. Soon they were both astride Kokiri's broom, posing in profile.

"Okay, you two, haven't you primped enough?"

Kokiri called to them as she bustled around. "Have a look at the western sky. There's barely any sunset left."

"Mom, can you make the skirt just a little shorter?" Kiki asked, hiking it up and standing on her tiptoes.

"Why? It looks good on you."

"I think it would be cuter if you could *actually* see my feet."

"This way is much more graceful. It's better to look mild-mannered. Of course, some people complain about witches no matter what you do. Now then, here's your lunch." Kokiri patted Kiki's shoulder and set a little bundle down next to her. "I used herbs so it won't go bad as fast. Don't eat it all in one place. I remember my mom did a great job making my coming-of-age lunch. She cast some spell on the herbs in the bread that kept it from going bad or even stale. It's a shame we don't know how to do that anymore."

"That seems like the sort of thing that would be easy to pass on, though," Okino chimed in, coming in from his study with a book in his hand. "I wonder why it disappeared. Maybe that's just the nature of magic?"

"It's strange that I'm a witch and even I don't know. Some say it's because there's no such thing as a completely dark night or perfect silence anymore—if there's a light on or if there's even a tiny noise, we get distracted and can't get our magic to work."

"Certainly compared to ancient times, it's gotten a lot brighter," Okino said. "Nowadays there's always a light on somewhere."

"Yes, the world sure has changed." Kokiri nodded, but Kiki, looking in the mirror, had a different idea.

"Hmm, you think that's why?" Kiki turned around with a dissatisfied frown. "I don't think it's the world's fault that magic has disappeared. Maybe people hold themselves back too much. Mom, aren't you always saying that witches must be quiet and modest? I hate the idea of living my life constantly worrying about what people will say—I'm going to do whatever I want!"

"Oh! That's quite a declaration." Okino's eyes widened dramatically.

"Listen, Kiki," Kokiri said. "In the past, it wasn't just us witches—all sorts of people had mysterious powers. But most regular people connected these gifts to bad things in their heads. They believed our powers would bring terrible luck."

"That could be true." Okino nodded thoughtfully.

"It was! You always heard about how witches made mold grow in fresh milk, but that was simply a way to make a special kind of cheese. And now look, today *everyone* eats that same cheese." As she spoke, Kokiri looked at Kiki with concern. "Witches were able to survive in that sort of world because we forged a give-and-take relationship with everyone else. Sometimes we hold back, but we also help each other out however we can. I think it was a good thing. Because of this, there are even people like your dad who research witches and fairies to gain a better understanding of us."

"Was that a compliment? What an honor." Okino jokily bowed.

"Oh, my goodness, it's pitch-dark outside." Kokiri

stood up and clapped her hands. "The moon'll be out soon. We need to hurry up and eat. No more time for these complicated conversations."

"Full-moon nights are bright," Okino said, "so they should be good for leaving on a journey. But according to my research, the data also shows a fifty-fifty chance of rain on days witches have come of age—"

"That's just the luck of the draw. Tonight seems like it'll be fine. The air is so clear. Kiki, are you really ready to go?" Skillfully evading Okino's grumbles, Kokiri began to bustle around the room again.

"I hope you find somewhere nice to live." Okino looked Kiki in the eye.

"But, Kiki, you can't get impatient and settle without giving your choice proper thought," Kokiri called.

"I know. All you guys do is worry."

"It's not as if she's going to another planet," Okino said, trying to cheer both Kokiri and Kiki up. "It's just a different town. And after a year, you can come back home for a celebratory visit."

Kokiri stood before Kiki again with a serious expression on her face. "Kiki, I know I'm harping on this, but please choose your town carefully. Think twice about picking one that seems nice just because it's lively or has lots of shops. Big cities are often full of busy people who don't have time to care about anyone else. And when you arrive, don't be shy. Make sure to smile. You have to gain people's trust."

"I know, Mom. I'll be fine. Don't worry." Kiki nodded repeatedly, then turned to Okino. "Hey, Dad, do you remember when you used to hold me up high? You would put your hands under my arms and lift me up and down. Could you do it one more time?" She looked down quickly, a little embarrassed.

"Sure!" Okino replied with extra pep. He put his hands under her arms and tried to lift her. "Phew! You're heavy. When did you get so big? Let me try one more time." He staggered a bit but managed to raise her.

"I—I'm up! But—ha-ha-ha—it tickles!" Kiki squirmed and laughed.

Through the living room window, the light of the full moon poured over Mount Green in the east—just as they had expected.

"I guess I should get going." Kiki had planned on saying a proper goodbye, but all that came out was that simple line. She slung her bag over her shoulder and grabbed the broom that had been standing next to her. With her other hand, she picked up the red radio her father had bought for her. Then she looked at Jiji, who sat obediently at her feet. "Okay, say goodbye."

Jiji stood and looked up at Okino and Kokiri.

"We're counting on you, Jiji," said Kokiri.

As usual, he twitched his tail in reply.

"Well, Mom, I'll write a letter as soon as I get there."

"Yes, keep us posted."

"If it doesn't go well, you can always come home," added Okino.

"That's not happening!" Kiki hurriedly replied.

"Don't start going easy on her now." Kokiri shot a soft glare at Okino.

When Okino opened the door, voices shouting "Congrats!" came flying in. Ten townspeople were waiting at the gate!

Kiki was so surprised, she didn't know what to say.

"You knew she was leaving tonight?" Kokiri asked hoarsely.

"We can't let our little Kiki leave without saying goodbye."

"And it's something to celebrate."

"Come back and ring the bells now and then."

"Bring us stories."

"Aw, thanks, everybody." Kiki finally managed to squeeze that much out, then lifted Jiji to hide her crumpling face.

"I'm glad the weather's good," Okino said quietly, looking up at the sky.

After exchanging goodbye after goodbye, Kiki hung her radio from the front of her broom, sat Jiji on the back, and jumped on. Once the broom was hovering, she turned around. "Take care, Mom," she said to Kokiri from a few feet above. If she flew any closer, she knew they would both end up crying.

"Make sure to look where you're going!" Kokiri's usual scolding voice sounded after her, followed by a burst of laughter from the townspeople. Kiki was relieved that her mom remained the same, even on this special occasion.

After one final "Goodbye!" she rocketed into the air. Gradually, everyone's waving hands below grew harder to see, and all the lights of the town twinkled like a starry night turned upside down. The full moon hung in the sky, watching over Kiki. Eventually even the lights of the town faded, and all she could see below were mountains shaped like the dark backs of animals.

"Hurry up and decide which way we're going," Jiji prodded behind her.

"Umm . . ." Kiki looked in all four directions, flustered. "South, I want to go south. I heard that if you keep going south, you eventually reach the sea, and I want to see the sea at least once. Is that all right with you, Jiji?"

"Am I allowed to say no?"

"Please don't," she yelled, and shook the broom a bit.

"Then why ask me at all?" Jiji huffed. "Anyway, I'm begging you not to mess this up. We're looking for a town, not the sea, remember."

"Yes, I understand that. Okay, south, south . . ." She looked here and there, then sighed with relief. "Got it! It's this way. The moon is on my left, so there's no mistake."

With a whistle she accelerated, flying faster and faster. The wind blowing past her grew stronger, and the bristles of her broom sounded like a running river. Now and then she saw a scattering of lights between the dark mountains. Sometimes she came upon gray-colored fields, but that didn't happen very often. Mostly it was mountain after mountain.

Kiki flew on and on. Faintly, the eastern sky began to grow lighter. Then bright light spread rapidly, chasing the darkness away, and the world that had been gray and navy burst into all sorts of colors. The hills were carpeted in the gentle greens of spring and looked light enough to float into the air. Pointy, rocky mountain peaks gleamed dewily. Kiki's heart pounded—she was impressed that a single ray of sun could make the world this beautiful.

In a small valley, she saw a village with trails of smoke rising from chimneys. Before long, she found a narrow stream glittering between the mountains. Sometimes it snaked out of sight before showing itself again, growing bigger and bigger as it went on.

"Let's try flying along this river," she suggested. "Rivers supposedly end at the sea."

Kiki flicked on her radio and whistled along to the music. Her broom was catching a favorable breeze and cruising at a nice pace.

"You know, Mom was saying big cities can be hard, but I really don't want to live in a tiny town," Kiki said to herself.

"Then what kind of town sounds good?" Jiji raised his voice over the wind and the radio.

"One bigger than Mom's. With tall buildings, a zoo, and a station with trains coming and going. Oh, and an amusement park! What about you, Jiji?"

"You're awfully greedy. As long as I have a sunny roof, and a sunny bay window, and a sunny hallway—"

"Are you cold?" Kiki interjected.

"Yeah, a little."

"Then come over here. Don't be afraid to tell me what you need. It's just us two now," she said, taking Jiji from where he clung to her back and putting him in her lap.

"Hey, Kiki, how about that town?" Jiji asked after a while, abruptly poking his head out. The town directly below them was shaped like a round dish and surrounded by pretty green hills. From above, the clusters of orange and green roofs looked like carrots and peas in a soup.

"Seems nice," Kiki said.

"This type of place is probably good to live in, you know?" Jiji said, putting on a knowledgeable air.

"But isn't it kind of small? Wait, look over there!" Kiki suddenly pointed with a shout. Far below was a little black dot that seemed to be coming toward them. When she took a closer look, she realized it was a witch with a black cat on her shoulder. But this witch flew in herks and jerks as if she were riding an unruly horse.

"Let's go say hello." Kiki aimed her body down.

"Oh!" Still herking and jerking, the other witch widened her eyes when she saw Kiki. Age-wise, she could have been Kiki's big sister. "Well, it's been quite a while since I met one of my own. Where did you come from? Could it be that today is your special day?" the witch said, looking Kiki up and down.

"That's right. I just left last night. You could tell?" Kiki steered her broom to fly alongside her.

"Of course I can tell! You look so dressed up, and your face is all tense. I was just like you once!"

"I'm tense, huh? I thought I was pretty relaxed, but . . ." Kiki giggled. "When did you come of age?"

"Almost exactly a year ago."

"How do you like this town?" Kiki pointed below.

"I'm finally used to it."

"It was pretty tough?" Worried, Kiki looked away.

"It wasn't so bad." The big-sister witch shrugged proudly, and dimples appeared in her cheeks. She had a kind face.

Kiki remembered Kokiri's advice about smiling. *So that's the face I need.*

"What do you do for a living?"

"I'm a fortune-teller—with my cat, Pupu, here. I can tell how people are feeling, and I have a reputation for being right. They might just be flattering me, but, well, the townspeople are friendly."

"Nice. And you get to go visit your parents soon, right?"

"Yes, that's right! I can return with my head held high, so I'm satisfied. It may not look like it, but things are hard sometimes."

"I believe it. Seems like your broom is broken, too."

The big-sister witch laughed. "Ha! It's not. I'm just bad at flying. But if you don't fly every now and then, you start to forget you're a witch, and even who you are at all—can't have that. Anyway, today I'm going to a ranch over the mountain because one of their cows is in a bad mood. That's why I'm up and out so early this morning. It's not *really* fortune-telling, but . . ."

"Wow, you're going to see a cow?"

"The trick to working as a witch is to take every job. This cow is a little strange, almost like a human. The other day she was complaining that she didn't like the sound of the bell around her neck."

"Wow, how spoiled." Kiki laughed.

"Maybe she's into music? Changing her bell and singing to her for a bit put her in a better mood. And the owner of this cow treats me to the most delicious cheese as a thank-you. It smells so good, and when you grill it, it gets all stretchy and gooey. I'm really looking forward to having some more."

"It's great that things seem to be going so well for you. I'm jealous."

"You'll do fine. You're cute like me, and you seem fairly smart like me, too. Plus you're good at flying. You do seem a bit on the feisty side, but, well, I'm sure you'll do your best. Anyhow, I'm in a hurry, so see you!"

The big-sister witch waved and herked and jerked off into the distance.

"She was pretty braggy," Jiji said in a low voice.

"But she complimented me."

"Maybe. But her cat was so aloof. He didn't even say hello, just acted all smug because he's a little older."

"Oh, so *you* wanted to talk to *him*, Jiji? If you felt that way, you should have said something."

"Well, it's not like I wanted to . . . ," Jiji muttered.

"Anyhow, I've got my own things to figure out." Kiki speedily reversed and continued her journey.

As she flew on, she passed a few towns that seemed nice. Each time, Jiji would prod, "Why not make up your mind now?" But Kiki insisted on going to the sea.

"Just a bit farther. Only a little," she kept repeating.

Eventually there were fewer mountains, and in their place, more fields, villages, and towns began to appear. By this point, the river was wide and flowed in big twists and turns. Kiki and Jiji's little shadow across the water looked just like a fish swimming below the surface.

"Oh, isn't that the sea?" Jiji shouted.

Kiki had been distracted by the view below, but when she looked up, she saw a line of light off in the distance separating the blue sky from the water.

"Yeah, that's the sea for sure. You noticed it right away!"

"What, so it's just a big puddle?" Jiji seemed dissatisfied.

"No, it's amazing! It's wonderful, isn't it?" Kiki shouted in utter delight as she gazed as far as her eyes could see up and down the coast. Suddenly she noticed a town right where the river emptied into the sea. "A town! Oh, look, a big bridge!" she shouted again.

"Oh, a train!" Jiji exclaimed at the same time.

"Let's check it out!" Kiki sped ahead on her broom.

When they were closer, she realized the town was even bigger than she thought. Tall buildings, both box-shaped and triangular, jutted toward the sky. Kiki took a sweeping look around and exclaimed, "This is the place!"

"You don't think it's too big?" Jiji seemed a little worried. "Remember what Kokiri said, to think twice about big, busy towns."

"I like it here. Look, see that over there?" She pointed at a clock tower near the center of town, a tower so tall it seemed like a ladder to the heavens. "Wouldn't it be fun to grab that and twirl this place like a spinning top? Its shadow stretches so far, it's like the whole town is a sundial." Kiki peered down with starry eyes.

"You seem awfully excited," Jiji said. "But there could be a witch already living here, like that other town before."

"Well, we won't know until we land and ask."

Kiki sharply angled her broomstick down and landed lightly on one of the town's roads.

On the ground, the streets were bustling with afternoon shoppers. When Kiki jumped onto the cobblestones with a thud, everyone was startled. Some people seemed scared and fled, while others hid behind someone else. Soon Kiki was surrounded by a wall of people. She hurriedly took the broom out from between her legs, placed Jiji on her shoulder, and put on a cheerful smile.

"Um, I'm Kiki, and I'm a witch—"

"Oho, a witch, huh?" one older woman said. "You're a rare breed these days." The woman adjusted the glasses on her nose and stared.

"So there's no witch in this town? Phew! Well, as I was saying, I'm Kiki the witch, and this is my black cat, Jiji. I'll make myself at home," she said as she looked around at everyone and then curtsied more carefully than usual.

"Make yourself at home? You mean *here*, in the town of Koriko?" a man chimed in.

"Who made that decision?" a woman exclaimed. "Was it that new mayor?"

At this point, everyone was exchanging glances with the people next to them and chatting among themselves.

"Is there anything good about having a witch around?"

"Isn't it kind of strange to go flying about the sky in this day and age?"

"They say there used to be one here long ago, but we've been fine without one all this time."

"Mommy, witches use magic, right? Seems cool!"

"They do outrageous things! You'll get scared!"

"Do you have some wicked plot?"

As Kiki listened to all the comments, which couldn't really be called kind, her chest tightened. Even so, she tried to be confident. *Smile, smile,* she thought. She needed to come up with a reply.

"I'd love to live in this town. It's pretty, and I like the clock tower," Kiki complimented them.

"Well, it's great that you've taken a liking to the town, but . . ."

"But we don't want any trouble."

"Whatever floats your boat."

Once everyone was satisfied, having had their say, they scattered every which way and disappeared back into the town.

All Kiki's energy had disappeared, leaving her discouraged. When she had heard that the city didn't have a witch, she'd hoped the townspeople would find her interesting and welcome her. But now the exhaustion from flying since morning on an empty stomach hit her, and she felt like sinking into a pit.

The people from Kiki's hometown were happy to live near a witch. They valued her family, and even said kind things like *Witches are like oil for your gears* and *Having a witch around brings life to the town.* Every day someone was stopping by offering something tasty, saying, *I just had a little extra!* And naturally, Kiki and her family gave back. They shared Kokiri's sneeze medicine, taught the townspeople the names of traditional herbs, played cat's cradle with elderly folks who lived alone, delivered lost and forgotten items by broom—it was a give-and-take lifestyle, just as Kokiri said.

That was how it had been ever since Kiki was born, so this *whatever floats your boat* attitude was strange. After all, Kiki was new to town and she had just come of age—how was she supposed to "float her boat"?

Kiki moved to the side of the road and trudged along sadly, dragging her broom.

"It's just like Kokiri said. Big towns are no good," Jiji murmured into her ear from where he was still perched on her shoulder.

Kiki nodded slowly so her tears wouldn't overflow. "What should we do?" she whispered, petting Jiji.

"Things will work out somehow." He flicked his tail back and forth with extra energy.

It was almost nighttime. Kiki still had plenty of the food from Kokiri left, but she wasn't sure what to do about a place to sleep. Even if she had money for an inn, was there a place in this town that would let her stay? Her confidence shattered, Kiki helplessly roamed the streets.

"Psh!" Jiji abruptly shouted, trying to cheer Kiki up. "Witches have gotten so wimpy. In the olden days, everybody in this place would have had to watch their backs. An old-school witch would have picked the whole town up by the clock tower and stuck it on a mountain somewhere."

Kiki shrugged slightly and said nothing. She wasn't sure where they were going, but after wandering for a while, they found themselves on a narrow street. Instead of tall buildings, it was lined with little houses that seemed to lean over the road. At some point the sun had set, and the shops on either side had closed their doors. From the clinking of dishes and laughter that echoed on the other side of the windows, it sounded like dinnertime.

Suddenly, she heard a woman's high-pitched voice coming from inside a half-closed bakery.

"Oh goodness, that lady forgot something awfully important! Dear, go and take this to her, why don't you?"

Kiki thought perhaps the woman was talking to her and stopped. But soon after, she heard a man's voice.

"'Awfully important'? What are you fussing about—it's just the baby's pacifier. It's not as if she forgot the baby. I've got a get-together tonight. I'll run it over in the morning."

"But I'm telling you, that's not good enough. She's a very good customer. She comes from so far away—with her baby in tow—to buy our butter rolls. You say it's 'just' a pacifier, but to a baby, it's important—as important as your pipe is to you! The poor thing won't be able to sleep tonight! If you're not going, then I will."

The woman, who must have been the owner of the bakery, came out from behind the door. The man shouted after her.

"Hey, you can't do that! Cross the big river in your condition?"

Kiki saw the woman had a huge tummy, like a baby might be born at any minute. A rubber pacifier was clenched in her hand.

Turning around, the woman called, "Then are you going to go for me?"

"Tomorrow I will," the man replied.

"Hmph." She stuck her chin out. "You're going to be a father soon yourself. I can't believe my baby will have such a grump for a dad."

After shouting at him, she gathered her protruding belly in her hands and set off walking. Her shoulders swayed back and forth, and her breath came roughly.

Without thinking, Kiki called out after her. "Excuse me! If you don't mind me going, I'll deliver it for you."

The woman turned around and backed up a couple of steps. Then she gave Kiki a quick look, head to toe.

"You're such a young lady, but you're wearing black clothes and carrying a broom—are you a chimney sweep?"

"No, actually I—I just came to this town, and I'm a witch," Kiki said nervously.

The lady ran her eyes over Kiki again. "You don't say! Wow, a witch, huh? I've heard about them before, but it's my first time seeing one." She heaved a sigh. "But are you pulling my leg? You must be from a theater troupe or something, right?"

Kiki hurriedly shook her head. "No, I'm really a witch! So if you need something delivered, I can do it easy-peasy. Please, let me help you," she offered politely.

"A real witch, you say? Well, delivering it will be a bit of a trip. Is that all right with you?"

"Sure, I don't mind going any distance. Although if it's too far north . . . it's not up by the North Pole, is it? My dress isn't very warm, and I don't have a cape."

The lady burst out laughing. "I think I like you. So you'll do it, then?"

"Yes, of course." Kiki smiled and nodded. Then she suddenly grew worried. "Um, ma'am?"

"Ack, don't 'ma'am' me!" The lady put her palms

up to ward off the formality. "I'm a baker, and the name's Osono."

"Then, uh, Mrs. Osono, I'm going to fly it over. Is that all right?"

"Now you're going over the top. You don't need to take an airplane!"

"No, I'm going to take my broom."

"What?" Osono cocked her head and worked her mouth open and closed until she could finally utter, "This sure is a strange day." Then she shook her head clear and said, "You can be a witch or a scarecrow, you can fly or swim—it's all fine by me. I don't like to make things too complicated. What's important right now is delivering the pacifier."

"Hearing you say that puts me at ease." Kiki grinned. Jiji waved his tail charmingly from her shoulder.

"If that's the case, then let's get this done as soon as we can," Osono said, digging around in the pocket of her apron. "I'll draw you a map. Also, it's not that I don't trust you, but once you've delivered it, have the baby's mother write her name on this. When you bring it back, I'll be waiting with something to thank you."

"Wonderful!" Kiki shouted. Then she took the map and the pacifier, mounted her broom, kicked off the ground, and climbed into the sky.

"You really are a witch, huh?" Kiki heard Osono's surprised voice at her back as she flew away.

When Kiki arrived with the pacifier, the baby was wailing. But once his mother popped the pacifier in, he smiled. The baby's mother was very appreciative and signed the map at Kiki's request. "You really helped me out," she said, and thanked Kiki over and over.

Kiki felt incredible as she flew back to the bakery, and hearing that she had "really helped" breathed new hope into her discouraged heart. "You know," she told Jiji, "I'm feeling all right. So you can feel better, too."

"Hmph," he sniffed. "Jeez, I'm starving all of a sudden."

"Me too!" Kiki reached out and patted Jiji's stomach as they continued on her broom. "Once this errand is done, let's go find a tree to sit under and eat the lunch Mom packed for us—but only a little. We have to make it last. I'm glad the moon is shining so bright tonight."

Osono the baker was still standing in the same place Kiki left her, looking up at the sky with her mouth hanging open. Once Kiki quietly landed, Osono blurted, "Flying really is handy, huh? Will you please teach me how?"

"That's impossible. If you don't have witch blood in you, you won't be able to fly."

"Oh," Osono said disappointedly. "But we don't know for sure that I don't. What do you think? Do I look part witch?" She let her belly go, then spread her arms and flapped them like bird wings.

Kiki looked away and laughed a little. "As I thought, it seems you're not a witch."

"As you thought? How can you tell?"

"I just can, I suppose."

"Well, that's no fun. But you're right—it's probably impossible. I never heard anything about my grandma or any great-grandmas being witches. Anyway, how was the baby?"

Kiki handed her the map with the mother's signature. "He was crying, but he cheered up right away. It made me happy, too."

"That's great! Okay, then, Miss Witch, I need to thank you."

"Please call me Kiki. And I don't need anything in return. I'm happy to have met someone so nice. That's more than enough. Like I said, I just arrived in town."

"My, how humble," Osono said. "Well, I'm sorry I only have the things that didn't sell today, but . . ." She handed Kiki a bag holding five butter rolls.

"Ooh, these look delicious. I'm happy to take them," Kiki said breathlessly. Then she gave a polite curtsey and turned to go.

"Hey, Miss Witch—your name is Kiki, you said? You just got to this town, right? Where are you staying?"

Kiki turned around, cuddling Jiji, and lowered her eyes.

"Surely you have somewhere to stay!" Osono demanded. Kiki remained silent.

"*What?* You have to speak up about things like that! In that case, use the second floor of our flour house. It's small, but it has a bed and running water."

"Really?" Kiki shouted, squeezing Jiji without thinking.

"If you don't like it, you can look for a better place tomorrow."

"Oh, I definitely won't do that. Thank you so much! But are you sure it's all right? I'm a witch, and it seems people in this town don't like us very much." Kiki hung her head again, but Osono took her chin in her hand, brought her head up, and gave her a wink.

"I've taken a shine to you. Don't worry. Plus, I think there's something a little bit wonderful about having a witch stay at our place."

The flour house, which was right next to the bakery, really *was* a flour storehouse, and it seemed completely coated in the white powder. After Kiki and Jiji relaxed and ate some of their food, they crawled into bed, exhausted.

"I might be a white cat by tomorrow." Jiji looked himself over and sneezed.

"But look, Jiji! There's a bay window that will get a lot of sun, just like you wanted."

After such a long trip, Kiki was relieved that her coming-of-age day was finally drawing to a close.

"Hey, Kiki, should we look for a different town tomorrow?" Jiji asked.

"I think I'm going to stay here a little longer. I

wasn't welcomed exactly as I hoped, but the baker likes me, right? There might be another person who does, too, don't you think?"

"Well, yeah. There might even be three." As quickly as Jiji answered, he was soon snoring the even breaths of sleep.

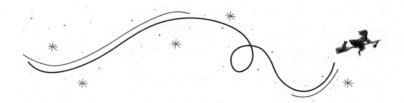

KIKI OPENS A SHOP

Three days had passed since Kiki the Witch moved to the town of Koriko.

Taking full advantage of Osono's offer to stay as long as she liked, Kiki holed up in the flour house. She sat in a daze on the edge of the bed, sometimes eating bits of the leftover lunch from her mother or the bread from Osono, even though she didn't have much appetite. As if her nerves were contagious, Jiji was glued to her side.

Today Kiki needed to go out to buy food, but she couldn't get herself to leave her room. The unending clamor of the city and the sight of the busy-looking people hurrying past her window scared her. Everything in this town seemed to operate in a mechanical way. The night she'd delivered the pacifier, she had regained a bit of confidence, but by the next day, those feelings had completely vanished.

All morning, Kiki repeated half-hearted excuses in her head.

Well, because . . .

I just . . .

I mean . . .

She could stay in the town and pretend to be human, or if she swallowed her pride, she could even go home. *But then I'll be just like a snail stuck in my shell my whole life. Apologies to snails, but I don't want to be like that!*

Kokiri's broom stood in the corner of her room, and Kiki stared at it with one hand on her chest.

This is no good. I need to find a job I can do. It's just like Mom said. In a big city, everyone is busy, and here I am in the middle of one. I delivered that pacifier. Maybe I can do more tasks like that? I'm good at flying, and there might be lots of people who don't have time to run a little errand.

As she thought about this, Kiki started to perk up.

So when Osono came to check on her, she asked for advice on her new idea.

"Deliver things? You mean like a transportation service?" Osono asked, not quite understanding.

"Yes, but the things I transport wouldn't be big enough to call cargo exactly—just lots of little things, sort of casual. Like, you know, people could ask me for favors the same way they might ask their neighbor."

"Hmm, that could be something. Come to think of it, that would help *me* out. Once the baby is born, it'll be hard for me to run even a quick errand. Yeah, I think this'll be good!" Osono leaned closer. "But for such small things, it'll be difficult to set prices. What's your plan?"

"Oh, just a little of whatever people have is fine."

"What do you mean?"

"Sharing whatever you have. That's how we get by as witches. We make ourselves useful to people with whatever skills we have, and in return, people share what they have with us. It's what you call give-and-take." Without even realizing it, Kiki was starting to sound like Kokiri.

"Oh, now that you mention it," Osono said, "I've heard of that before. But that won't be enough, will it?"

"It will—witches don't need much. You can see

how simple my clothes are, and I don't eat a lot. My plan is to just accept that if I don't have something, I probably don't need it."

"So that's how you'll make this work?" Osono nodded, impressed. "Then you'll need a storefront, huh?"

"Yes, something small, even just a sign that says 'Courier' or something."

"How about here? The first floor of the flour house," Osono offered. "I can organize our things into one corner."

"What? Are you sure?"

"Well, it might be too small. But it's smart to start small. Then you'll have the fun of watching your business grow." Osono seemed so excited, it was almost as if *she* were the one opening the shop. "Once you've decided, it's best to get going right away. But 'courier' might not be the best name. Sounds too much like 'worrier.' I think you can just call it a delivery service—I've heard that before. Or something like 'Speedy Home Deliveries' because you deliver right to people's homes in a timely fashion. Also, since you're the one doing the deliveries, you should add your name. 'Kiki's Delivery Service' sounds good, right?"

"Do you think including my name is a smart idea?"

"Don't be so modest. Having a unique name is best. Take a look at ours—Rock, Paper, Pastries. Sticks in your head! That's one trick to doing business." Osono eyed Kiki and nodded confidently.

The next day, Osono happily gave birth to a baby girl. Kiki was very busy helping with the bakery and looking after Osono, so prepping her shop was pushed off. Still, ten days later, she was ready to open.

She washed the floury front wall and hung up a sign. KIKI'S DELIVERY SERVICE—I DELIVER ANYTHING DOOR TO DOOR FASTER THAN ANYBODY ELSE! CALL 1-800-KIKI-CAN! The cute phone number was Osono's idea. Kiki and Jiji kept going outside to look up at the sign. "We're already open, so I guess there's no point in worrying now," Kiki murmured to herself.

"That's right." Jiji did his best to be encouraging. "Now, where's that girl who was so excited about coming of age?"

Inside, Kiki had everything she needed to run her shop, thanks to Osono's husband. He had moved all the bags of flour into a corner and built her a desk out of bricks and boards near the entrance. He put a brand-new red telephone on top and hung a big map of Koriko on the wall facing it. They polished the pillar people would see when they first walked into the shop till it shone, and then she hung her mother's broom there. Looking at it, she thought, *I'm glad I didn't bring that new slender broom. I have enough worries without flying on a stranger.*

A whole week went by without a single customer.

When Kiki went to visit the baby, Osono apologized. "Maybe using your name wasn't a good idea. I'm sorry. This is all my fault. Word travels fast here, and apparently some people heard you're a witch. Unfortunately, they worry you'll put a spell on their packages and they'll transform or disappear. I'm sure if they hired you once, they'd be hooked. If I could be out and about, I would help you."

"It's all right. I'm sure people will come around soon." Kiki forced a smile.

But when she sat at her desk, she was so upset she forgot to eat lunch. "It makes me so sad," she told Jiji. "Why do they assume witches will do something wicked?"

"Because they don't know better," he replied with a mature air. "It's nothing you can fix."

"It's true—they really have no idea. Witches have never done anything wrong. They might be different, but humans are so quick to decide that anything they don't understand is evil. I thought that was an old-fashioned idea, but—"

"So you have to show them. In other words, you need to advertise."

"Advertise? How?"

"Maybe write lots of letters."

"What kind of letters?"

"Explaining how you're a cute, helpful little witch."

"Hmm, that might work." Kiki finally brightened up a bit. "I guess I'll try it."

She stood and opened the window, and a gentle spring breeze blew in as if it had been waiting for the chance. When it brushed her face, all the tense feelings inside her melted away. She took a slow look around, like a mole that had just come out of its burrow, blinking in the sunlight. All the houses across the street had their windows wide open, too. Their curtains were tied back, allowing the sun to stream in. She heard the sound of a radio on the breeze, and then someone's voice calling out.

Suddenly her eyes landed on the window of a building a short way down the street. A young lady was waving her hands: *Here, over here, come over!* She motioned insistently, and no matter how Kiki looked at it, the gesture was directed at her.

Me? she asked, pointing at herself.

Yes! The lady nodded. Kiki quickly took in the view and counted—the lady was in a room on the second floor, four buildings over.

When Kiki went inside and up the stairs, a door was already open, so she assumed she had the right place. In the apartment, the waving lady stood in front of a mirror and was putting on a red hat with one hand and holding a sky-blue suitcase in the other.

"Oh, come in, come in!" She spoke rapidly when she noticed Kiki in the reflection. "I heard about you from the baker. You deliver things?"

"Yes, I do."

"She said you fly?"

"Yes." Kiki lowered her eyes, worried the lady was going to complain.

"She said all you need in return is a little something?"

Kiki nodded.

"You sure are adorable, though. I always thought witches had fangs and horns." She sounded surprised, but her expression was bored.

Kiki nearly shouted *That's not a nice thing to say!* but managed to catch herself. The woman must have noticed her reaction.

"Sorry. It's just that we've never had a witch in this town, you know? At least, I haven't seen one before. And they're always so scary in stories! By the way, how much counts as 'a little something'? If you fly, it must be expensive."

"No, just a little of whatever you have is enough."

"Whatever I 'halve'? Half of what? I mean, I'm a seamstress, so I could halve the length of your skirt. I'm taking up and letting down hems all the time."

The lady turned around for the first time and looked Kiki up and down, wrinkling her nose. Then she shook her head, clucking her tongue in disapproval. "Tsk, tsk, tsk. That dress is cute, but it's a bit long, isn't it? The style these days is to show your knees. Ah, yes, that's the perfect trade! I'll be back in three days, and then I'll take your hem up. Why don't we have that be your fee?"

I don't even know what I'm delivering yet and you're already deciding the fee?

Kiki stood there frowning a little. The lady looked in the mirror and pinned on her hat, then spoke even faster than before.

"I got called by a client far away and have to race over there. Once she decides she wants a dress, she needs me to come right away—so impatient."

The lady pointed at a birdcage covered in white lace sitting on a table. "This is a present for my nephew's fifth birthday, and I'd like you to deliver it for me. He said he wanted a new birdcage and a stuffed toy. He made me promise I'd deliver it today by four o'clock. If it's even a little late, he said he'll make me do ninety-four headstands. Just try doing that many! You'll forget which end is your head and which is your feet. There's only an hour left. Don't be late! I'm begging you. The address is Ten Apricot Street. If you go up the river, it's the road behind the big flower shop on the outskirts of town. The name—they'll understand if you say 'Buzzcut Buster.' Okay, thanks in advance."

When she'd finished her mile-a-minute explanation, she rushed Kiki out of the apartment, handing her the covered birdcage with the stuffed toy, and then left herself.

Kiki flipped up the lace and looked inside the cage. "Oh, Jiji, he looks just like you. How adorable."

Sitting on a silver cushion inside the cage was a stuffed black cat with a mint-green ribbon tied in a big bow around its neck.

Kiki put her broomstick through the handle of the birdcage so it was positioned right behind her and her radio. "Keep a close eye on it," she told Jiji as she sat him on the broom's bristles. Then she zoomed off.

"Been a while since I've flown!" Kiki exclaimed. "It feels so good."

The sun was already shining brightly in the western part of the sky. Now and then, the wind flipped up the lace covering the cage and Jiji stared in.

"Look at him, wearing a ribbon, all fancy like," he grumbled. Then, a moment later, he muttered to himself, "Perched on that *thing*."

"Oh, do you want a cat cushion, too?" Kiki turned around and smiled at him. "How are you jealous of a stuffed animal that can't even move around?"

Jiji ignored her and slowly crept closer to the cage. Then he extended a paw and pulled it closer with his claws. The broom jolted with a wobble.

"No! Hold still!" Kiki yelled.

Jiji pricked his ears up and pulled his paw back to his mouth.

"Jiji, do you want to go in the cage? Seriously?"

"I mean, it's so pretty."

"Ugh, Jiji, sometimes I can't believe we're the same age."

She smiled at how ridiculous he was being. The broom began to fly smoothly again. But as if he had been waiting for that moment, Jiji swiftly clawed the door open and tried to climb into the cage. The broom wobbled horribly.

"Eek!" Kiki rushed to grab the broom, but before she had the chance, the stuffed cat spilled out of the open cage. "Oh no!" It didn't matter if she screamed or reached out her hand—it was too late. The stuffed toy spun like a black pinwheel as it fell from the sky.

Kiki immediately swooped after it. The leafy green forest below grew closer and closer, until Kiki plunged in, tree branches whipping her body. Eventually she found a little clearing and touched down. Then she got straight to searching, waving her broom to look through the bushes and tall grasses as she walked along.

But she couldn't find the cat. The forest was huge, and the trees were covered in soft leaves. If the toy had gotten caught in the canopy of tangled branches above, she would never be able to find it. On top of that, the stuffed animal was light, so the wind could have blown it in an entirely different direction.

Kiki wanted to cry.

That lady had believed in her, though it was the first time they'd met, and trusted her with this important delivery. This was Kiki's first customer since the shop opened, and the job was going to end in failure.

It was almost four o'clock. Kiki glared at Jiji, who was hunched over with guilt.

"What am I gonna do with you?" Almost immediately, she gasped. "Oh, I thought of a great idea! Jiji, you get in the cage instead."

Jiji gazed up and backed away, shaking his head.

"You were the one who wanted to go inside. Just get in there. We're out of time." Kiki raised her voice and pointed at the cage. Her eyebrows angled in a way that meant business.

Jiji raced into the cage and sat on the silver cushion, which was still inside. Kiki closed the door and spoke gently. "It's just for a little while. As soon as I find the toy, I'll come back and swap you out."

He looked up at her with regret in his eyes. "So *I'm* a stuffed animal now?"

"That's right."

"I can't meow?"

"Nope. Just go to sleep. That'll be the easiest."

"Can I breathe?"

"As little as possible."

"But this is horrible. I'm up against Buzzcut Buster. That lady said he would make her do ninety-four headstands!"

"You'll be fine. I'll come back for you as soon as I can."

Jiji sighed, curled up into a sad little ball, and turned away from Kiki. This time she carefully hung the birdcage in front of her before taking off in a hurry.

Kiki flew along the river, checking the names of the streets at each intersection, and she had no trouble finding 10 Apricot Street behind the flower shop. When she rang the doorbell, she heard thudding footsteps. Then the door swung open.

"Auntie?"

Standing in front of Kiki was a boy with one bandage on his cheek, one on his nose, two on his forehead, and three on his knees.

"I'm sorry. Your aunt couldn't come. But I came in her place. Here are the presents she promised you. Happy birthday!"

When the boy took the cage, he peered inside right away and then started jumping up and down, holding it tight. Through a gap in the lace, Kiki could see Jiji bouncing around inside with a grimace on his face.

"Oh, hey, hey," Kiki quickly said. "Be nice to the kitty, okay?"

"I will! I'll take good care of him. I'll fold him up properly and put him in my pocket." The boy stuck his tongue out.

"Eep!" A pitiful noise sounded from inside the cage.

"Well, see you later!" Kiki waved to the boy.

"Oh! Will you have something else for me?"

"Um, well, perhaps!" And with that, she mounted her broom and raced off.

When Kiki returned to the clearing, she realized the forest was actually part of a park. She took another careful walk around the area where the stuffed toy had fallen, but she couldn't find it anywhere. At this rate, she worried Jiji would remain with that "Buzzcut Buster" forever. He would never come home, even though they had just started life on their own as a pair.

Dusk approached, and Kiki leaned against a tree, at wit's end. She looked down and clutched the skirt of her dress. "The best option I have is to cut off the hem of my dress and make a stuffed black cat myself. I always wanted a shorter skirt, so I guess it's worth a try."

Just then, she faintly heard someone singing.

> *The bad black is a smoky black.*
> *The good black is a black-cat black.*
> *But the best of all is a witch's black.*
> *Blacks come in all different various hues,*
> *So come on now, you have to choose.*

Startled, Kiki whirled around and spotted a cottage beyond the tree she had been leaning against, behind a section of a hedge that had grown wild. The cottage window was open, and a woman with her hair tightly pulled back faced away from Kiki, painting a picture.

Maybe she saw something. I'll go ask.

Kiki made her way through a gap in the hedge and crossed the flowering lawn to approach the house.

When she peeked through the window to call out to the woman, she realized that the woman's picture was cat-shaped. With a start, she looked beyond the painting and gasped—it was the stuffed animal she had lost!

The woman heard her and turned around.

Face to face, they both shrieked.

"Ah, um, th-that—"

"Ah, that, y-you—"

"Oh, phew."

"Oh, good."

They both sighed in unison.

"I'm so glad I found it."

"I'm so glad I found it."

"What?"

"What?"

The two eyed each other, puzzled.

"For me, it's that black cat toy."

"For me, it's you—a girl in such a wonderful black dress."

Their voices overlapped and their sentences meshed into nonsense: *For me, it's that black girl wonder-cat dress toy.*

Kiki finally composed herself and asked the woman clearly, "Did that stuffed cat fall out of the sky, by any chance?"

The woman looked at Kiki curiously. "I don't know if it rained out of the sky or welled up out of the ground, but I found it in the forest a little while ago. I've been searching for a good black to paint for my exhibition. The real blackest black, you know? If possible, a witch's black. I'm just making do with the stuffed animal for right now." The woman stopped talking, but when she ran her eyes over the broom Kiki was holding, she yelped, "C-could it be that you're a—"

"Yes, I'm a witch."

The moment Kiki responded, the woman practically jumped out the window to grab her hand. "If you like," the woman said, "I'll give you this cat back.

But would you come inside and sit for me? I was even thinking about moving because I heard there hadn't been a witch in this town for ages. And now a witch has come to me! Come and sit, sit down."

Kiki was nearly swept up by the woman's momentum, but she flailed and said, "I will, I will. Just not right now. If I can have that toy, I'll bring back a real black cat—a witch's black cat! Then you can paint both of us."

"Really?"

"For sure!" Kiki shouted with a nod. Once she had the stuffed toy in hand, she rushed off without looking back.

"It's a promise, then!" the woman called after her.

By the time Kiki reached Buzzcut Buster's house, it was completely dark outside. Kiki tiptoed up to each lit window and peeked inside.

Oh, there's Jiji. He was in bed with Buzzcut Buster, who hugged him tightly.

Jiji was far from properly folded—he was crumpled. His face was turned toward his back, clamped down by the boy's hand, and his stomach was being crushed by the boy's arm. On his nose, he had a bandage that matched Buzzcut Buster's.

Kiki quietly opened the window, stood on her toes, and pulled Jiji's tail. Jiji didn't move. He'd kept his promise and truly transformed into a stuffed animal. The back of Kiki's nose stung as she held back tears of gratitude. *What a precious friend he is!*

"Jiji, Jiji," she called in a low voice. He slowly opened one eye. Kiki set the toy on the boy's stomach and whispered, "Hurry!"

Jiji slipped away from the boy and bounced like a ball into Kiki's arms. She couldn't tell if he was laughing or crying, but he was purring deep in his throat.

"How wonderful it is to breathe freely, to be able to move!" Jiji looked around with renewed curiosity as he and Kiki flew through the sky.

"About that," Kiki said without looking at him. "Sorry, but there's something else I need your help with. This time you don't have to pretend to be a stuffed animal, though. You can laugh, cry, whatever you like!"

"That'll be a piece of cake, then." Jiji nodded as if he understood everything perfectly.

But when the painter sat Kiki and Jiji down next to each other, she ordered, "Straighten up, Mr. Witch Cat. Curl your tail. And make a serious face. Okay, good, now hold your breath. Just like that, just like that—don't move!"

Jiji bristled angrily.

That only made the painter shriek with delight.

"Oh, fantastic! That's a witch's cat for you! Just like that, just like that."

As Kiki sat there prim and proper, she was thrilled. *There's another person who likes me!*

That night, Kiki wrote her first letter to Okino and Kokiri.

I decided to live in a place called Koriko. It's a big town near the sea. At first I thought it might be too big, but it's turned out to be perfect for the type of work I started to do. I started my own business: Kiki's Delivery Service.

She wrote about everything that had happened so far, leaving out the moments when she'd felt discouraged, of course. She ended her letter like this:

The seamstress said she would halve the length of my skirt, but I think I'm going to have her make a silver cushion for Jiji. Next time I'll send a picture of his calm face.

We're having fun, so please don't worry. Take care, both of you. Bye for now.

KIKI FINDS HERSELF
IN A TOUGH SPOT

Kiki opened the front door to her shop and instinctively shaded her eyes with her hand—*It's so bright!*

When she'd first arrived in town, the sun had beamed down with a mild, playful glow. It wasn't all that different from the sunlight in her small town back home with its many forests. But now it pounded down ruthlessly, as if taking aim and hurling itself.

"Summer by the sea is something else," Kiki murmured. "It's hard to breathe." She undid one of the buttons at her collar to cool off, then stood up on her toes.

Oh my gosh, it's not as if I'll be able to see the sea on tiptoe. I must be thinking of Mom's letter.

Back home, she would stand on tiptoe in her front garden, where she could see as far as the eastern peak of Mount Green. The note she received from Kokiri two days ago reminded her of the mountain and the little town she'd left.

Yesterday I was out, so I stopped by Mount Green on my way home. I remembered how when I would send you on an errand, you would stop off there and take forever to come back. The grass was almost up to my knees. I sat there for a while, looking up at the sky. And then what do you suppose happened? I fell asleep! The grass smelled so sweet, and the breeze was blowing so gently. I'm not sure how long I slept, but when I woke up, I rushed home. When your dad saw my face, he laughed. He said I looked just like you, with marks from the grass on my cheeks. I ended up laughing, too.

Kiki remembered playing on the fields of Mount Green under the blazing sun and walking the roads of her town. She missed it so much her heart ached.

"Okay," she said, shaking off the sad feelings. "Let's get the day started."

Switching gears, Kiki decided to polish her broom with a soft cloth. Caring for her equipment was something she had done every morning since opening her delivery service.

"Oh, what a busy bee you are. At it today, too?" Osono came out of the bakery next door carrying her baby and spoke to Kiki through the open window. "No matter how much effort you put in, I don't think you'll get much work today. The town is empty. Well, there does seem to be one determined boy cleaning the alley. But otherwise, there's almost no one around."

Kiki looked up and peered out at the street. Sure enough, all she could see was the high contrast of dazzling sunlight and black shadow.

"Today is Sunday," Osono explained. "Plus, it's the middle of the summer. Everyone's gone to the beach."

"The beach? Why?"

"To go swimming, of course. Why don't you take the day off and go, too?"

"But it's so hot."

"Oh, sheesh. That's the whole reason to go, isn't it?

It'll feel good. It's rough living here in the summer if you don't go to the beach."

"But I've never been swimming before."

"Even more reason to go. If you need a swimsuit, I'll lend you one. I happen to have a black one from when I was younger. Witches have to wear black, right?"

"But you're not going to come, Osono?"

"With the little one? I can't. I'll just have to suffer through the heat this year. You're lucky you can easily fly over."

"I'll go with you, though. I can watch the baby." Kiki reached through the open window and softly brushed the cheek of the child sleeping comfortably in Osono's arms.

"I'm fine. You haven't had any chance to relax since you got here. You've been getting more work little by little, so go take it easy for a change. You can simply lie on the sand. Wait just a minute and I'll grab the suit for you. If you wear it under your dress, it'll be easy to change when you get there." Osono bustled back into her house.

"The beach, huh?" Kiki murmured before turning to Jiji. "Should we go check it out?"

Jiji was lying like a pat of melted butter, sprawled on the steps in a shady spot where the breeze was better. He answered in a nasally, irked voice. "You're telling someone wearing a fur coat in this heat to *move*? How cruel!"

"But we'll be flying into the sea breeze. I think it'll feel much better than sitting at home. Plus, I need to take the broom out for a fun flight now and then."

"Now and then, huh?" Jiji sniffed and sluggishly rose to his feet, flicking his tail.

Kiki bobbed her head with a smile and set about closing the shop's windows.

When Osono brought the swimsuit, Kiki stretched it out first, then slipped it on. The fabric snapped back and clung to her skin like a rubber band.

"Is this how it's supposed to fit?" Kiki asked Osono, shrinking in embarrassment.

"Yes, you look great! I'm jealous of how well that suit fits you."

"It's like my body is *squished*—it feels weird."

"You're fine just as you are. Plus, once you get there, everyone will be wearing the same sort of thing. All right, get going!"

Kiki put her dress on over the swimsuit, and with her broom and radio in hand, she went outside with Jiji. Then she hung a sign on the door that said CLOSED TODAY.

Kiki and Jiji sped across the blue sky. The radio was playing a cheery song, and Kiki swayed to the music. "This feels great!" She skillfully caught the wind and flew side to side in big weaving curves. "Flying really is fantastic. It's no wonder Osono wanted to learn how."

Kiki squinted down at Koriko. The town spread like two butterfly wings from either side of the big river. It seemed to be moving to the music, too.

Jiji tapped her back. "Hey, Kiki, there's some kind of announcement on the radio."

At some point, a weather forecast had interrupted the music.

"We repeat this important warning. The gusts known as Mischievous Marine Winds may blow today off the coast of Koriko. True to their name, during this time of year, these winds come whipping through without warning. Everyone who is out swimming, please be careful."

"See, it's saying the weather's going to get bad," said Jiji.

"What? But it's so nice out!" Kiki wasn't worried at all. "Look, we can see the beach. There are plenty of people playing. The forecast must be a mistake. You always expect the worst when we're trying to have fun—it's a bad habit!"

"Being too giddy isn't a good habit, either." Jiji bristled and turned away.

A moment later, Kiki angled the broomstick to descend. She landed softly on an isolated patch of sand. Kiki had never heard of a witch going to the beach, so she thought it would be better to avoid sticking out.

Kiki sent a sidelong glance at the more crowded area. Everyone was absorbed in their fun. Some people were having sandball fights, while others were buried in sand up to their necks. Some were sunning their backs, some chased waves at the water's edge, and some swam in the ocean with big strokes. There were so many different things to do at the beach, and wherever she looked she found smiles and laughter.

The wind picked up and noisily whipped at the fabric of the beach umbrellas. The waves grew a little taller, too, and the shouts of the surfers grew more excited. Carrying the dress and shoes she had taken off, Kiki nervously hunched, hiding her body. It was her first time barefoot in sand, and though it wasn't even noon yet, the sand was so hot it was impossible to move slowly. She hopped along shrieking, and Jiji hopped too, sensibly trying to stay in Kiki's shadow. As they went, he grumbled, "We look ridiculous— like two beans in a frying pan. I wish we could show Kokiri."

When they finally made it to the crowded section of the beach, Kiki imitated the others by digging a hole and lying down in it on her stomach. Here, the sand was as warm and comforting as a bath, and it felt wonderful. All sorts of people's legs passed by. Kiki was relieved that everyone was too busy with their own fun to pay attention to anyone else. She propped her head up on her elbows and looked out at the sea. It was like a great, swelling creature in constant motion. People jumped in one after another, as if clinging to its back.

Kiki realized her mother hadn't told her anything about the sea. Perhaps it was only natural, since Kokiri had never seen it.

"Maybe I'll go in, too," she said to herself.

"Kiki, witches might melt or something if they go in water. Don't do it." Jiji eyed her anxiously.

"Look how much fun everyone else is having! I

don't think there's any reason it would be bad *just* for witches. I want to try dipping my feet in, at least."

As Kiki sat up on the sand, she spied a mass of black clouds on the horizon that hadn't been there before. Looking around, she watched little whirlwinds of sand spin by.

"Oh, maybe the weather forecast was right after all."

But the sun was still shining brightly overhead, so she gazed enviously back at the people playing in the water.

A voice called out nearby: "Hey!"

When Kiki turned, she saw a woman lying nearby on her stomach, smiling at her. The woman slowly sat up and pointed to the broom.

"Did you bring that all the way here to play with at the beach? Are you planning on using it instead of floaties?"

Kiki found the idea so silly she couldn't hold back her laughter.

The woman shrugged and laughed herself, then said, "I heard a witch came to town. I guess people are already copying her style—how cute! I'm so busy taking care of my son, I have no idea what the latest trends are. I saw a young man with one earlier, too."

Kiki hurriedly hid behind her broom.

"Look, there he is over there."

The woman pointed behind her. Kiki looked past the people playing in the sand and saw a boy carrying a bag and a broom, watching them.

"Oh, he's probably cleaning up the beach."

"Is that right? Are you a cleaner, too? I thought for sure . . ." As she spoke, she craned her neck and looked around. Then she suddenly shouted, "Hey! Hey, buddy, you can't go so far away! Stay where I can see you. Th-that's good, right there. You can splash in the water. Look, here comes a big wave."

When the woman waved, a little boy sitting on an orange inflatable raft kicked his feet. The woman turned back to Kiki and heaved a sigh.

"Kids are cute but such a handful. Being a mom is rough."

Then the woman looked away again and shrilly raised her voice. "Hey, don't go out too deep! That's right, sit right there! Good boy." She turned back to Kiki with a smile. "I'd at least like to get some relaxation time in when we come to the beach. Oh, do you think your little kitty would play with my son? He looks so sweet. Then my boy won't wander off." The woman reached out to pet Jiji, trying to get on his good side.

"Go play with him, Jiji." Kiki poked him in the tummy.

Jiji rose lazily and groaned from the pit of his stomach. "She called *me*—a full-grown cat—a 'little kitty.' Ugh," he grumbled to himself as he walked toward the water's edge, twitching his tail back and forth.

"What a smart kitty!" The woman watched with a smile until Jiji reached her son on the inflatable raft. Satisfied, she then lay back down on her stomach, humming.

Kiki decided to lie down, too. When she closed her eyes, she could hear the jumble of sounds around her more clearly. The sea's salty smell, a mix of fishiness and seaweed, was pretty nice, too.

Without warning, she heard a roar, and a completely different sort of wind blew past. It was so intense it seemed as though it fell from the sky. Yelps and screams of surprise rose along the beach.

After blinking the sand out of her eyes, Kiki saw straw hats crisscrossing through the air and inflatable rings rolling around like wheels. She stood up with a start. The peaceful beach had completely transformed. Some people grabbed their kids under their arms and ran for the pine grove at the end of the beach. Others were chasing belongings that blew in the wind.

"Oh no!" The woman next to her screamed at the top of her lungs, frantically sprinting toward the water.

Kiki's eyes followed the woman and she saw that the orange raft carrying the boy and Jiji was caught between two huge waves. The woman leaped into the water, but the raft, along with the boy and Jiji, was pulled into a strong whirlpool and dragged out to sea.

All Kiki could hear were piercing sobs. She ran toward the water and shouted to Jiji, "Hold on tight! I'm coming to save you!" Then she turned to the woman, who stood helplessly in the water. "Don't worry. I can fly. I'll save your boy."

Someone nearby said, "That's right. You're the flying girl from Kiki's Delivery Service, aren't you?"

"Please hurry," the woman urged. "Hurry!"

Kiki ran back to the sand to get her broom. But the moment she picked it up, she went pale. This wasn't her broom. It was a cheap one, a copy that looked nearly identical to her mother's.

How could this happen, especially at a time like this? Did someone swap my broom in the midst of this storm? Or was it while I was relaxing with my eyes closed? Kiki's heart pounded. *What do I do?*

In any case, she didn't have much time to think. Kiki mounted the unfamiliar broom in a hurry and took off. But the moment she was up, the broom took a nosedive, and she dipped into the water.

"Oh no!" everyone watching gasped.

Kiki pulled the handle up in a panic, but then the back bristles fell into the ocean with a *sploosh*. The broom grew heavier as it soaked up water, and drifted back toward the beach. Kiki tried everything she could to change direction, but the broom, unruly as a wild horse, kept pulling her backward and trying to throw her off. Meanwhile, the boy and Jiji drifted farther and farther away with each passing moment.

Still, Kiki desperately flew on. After being dunked and bucked along the way, she finally caught up to the raft. Then she stretched herself out on the broomstick and extended her hand. The boy was crying too hard to take it, so she finally managed to grab ahold of his trunks and lift him. Then she snatched Jiji by the tail. Right after she pulled them to safety, a huge wave crashed over the orange raft, sending it spinning and washing it away.

All the bystanders on the beach jumped up and cheered. When Kiki somehow made it back to shore, she handed the exhausted boy to his mother. Holding an equally exhausted Jiji, Kiki hurriedly pulled her dress on over her wet swimsuit. Then she grabbed her radio, hopped on the unsteady broom, and took off again.

"Why don't you rest for a bit," someone called to her. "This wind is bad!" But Kiki couldn't possibly do that. She needed to find her broom, and she had an idea of where to look. Earlier, she'd caught a glimpse of that boy who had a broom. He must have wanted a real one from a witch and swapped them! Kiki was furious. *It's unforgivable.* She was lucky she'd saved Jiji and the boy on the beach, but when she thought of what would have happened had she failed, she couldn't stop shaking. *I'm going to catch him and make him apologize a million times over.*

Kiki kept a careful watch on the ground as she continued herking and jerking across the sky on the bronco broom.

If someone wanted a witch's broom so badly they stole it, where is the first place they would go? Kiki thought it would be somewhere high, like a cliff—because, of course, they would want to try flying.

She flew from hill to hill between the beach and the town of Koriko.

"Kiki, over there!" Jiji pointed up ahead. Just as she thought, someone wearing a black dress was standing at the top of a little hill, about to test their flying skills. "Kiki, we have to stop them!"

"Shh! Quiet." Kiki stopped her broom in midair.

"They'll get hurt," Jiji warned again.

"If they want to fly, let's let them fly. If things turn out bad for them, they'll learn their lesson. Taking someone's belongings without asking is a horrible thing to do," Kiki replied coldly, holding the bucking broom steady.

"They're really gonna do it!" Jiji cried.

The person on the hill took a flying leap, but they landed flat on their bottom and rolled like a pebble down the slope.

Kiki flew after them. The broom thief was shaking their body out and rubbing their backside when she landed and teased irritably, "Too bad it didn't work out."

The face that looked up at her in surprise was— sure enough—the boy she had seen on the beach. He looked about Kiki's age. His glasses were cracked, and he was peppered with bleeding scrapes. Kiki giggled—he was even wearing a black dress identical to hers over his clothes!

"You sure put a lot of effort in," she said. "Right down to *my* witch dress."

The boy stood up with a frown, tore the dress off, blushed furiously, and hung his head.

"You caused a lot of trouble for me." Kiki thumped the handle of the broom into the ground, exaggerating her anger. In truth, seeing him imitate everything about her cracked her up more than it made her mad. "I'd like you to say you're sorry. At least a million times."

The boy said nothing as he backed away, bobbing his head apologetically.

"What's your excuse? Surely you weren't born yesterday, Mr. Thief."

"No, of course not. It was for research," the boy protested.

"What do you mean, 'research'?" Kiki raised her voice harshly.

"Don't yell like that—I'll tell you. My friends and I have an Aviation Club in town. We're trying to come up with new ways to fly. Right now, we're split into three groups in a research competition. One group is focusing on flying shoes, one is working on flying carpets, and the last one is doing witches' brooms."

"So you're in the broom group?" Kiki looked him directly in the eyes, and he blushed and nodded.

"That's why I was near your shop today. I heard you talking with the baker, and I rushed over to the beach to find you."

"You wanted to fly with my broom, huh? Well, it would never work. Even with the broom, you would never be able to fly. I can because I'm a witch. In other words, the blood running through here is different." Kiki thumped her chest once.

"So your *blood* makes you fly?" The boy's eyes widened as he looked at her.

"Ew. That's a weird way to say it." She burst out

laughing without meaning to, then composed herself and murmured with a straight face, "But I do wonder how it works. I don't know myself." She gazed up at the sky and cracked another smile. "But the broom makes a difference. If you're going to do research, at least use a broom that's easy to fly with. What *is* this thing?"

"It's no good? I made it. I tried to make it look like yours, but—"

"It's awful! It herks and jerks so much that my bottom hurts. If it were a horse, I would've tried to rein it in. And I embarrassed myself in front of all those people, too! Now give me my broom ba— Oh no!" Kiki wailed when she finally saw her broom. Her mother's hand-me-down lay on the ground, snapped in two. "What'll I do?" She picked up the pieces and cradled them.

"Sorry." The boy plunged his head down in apology.

"This was my mom's broom. She gave it to me when I left home, and it was so easy to fly on . . . ," Kiki said, her voice full of tears.

"Sorry," the boy said again in a tiny voice. Then he stood there with his shoulders slumped, hanging his head.

"Oh well," Kiki finally said hoarsely. She might

not have liked it, but there was nothing she could do about it, so she pushed the tears that threatened to overflow back down into her heart. "I'll make my own broom. I've made one before, so I think it'll work out. I doubt it'll go as smoothly as this one right from the start, but I'll master it eventually."

"I—I've studied a lot about how to fly smoothly, so there might be a way I can help you," the boy offered timidly.

"I appreciate the thought, but this is a job for a witch," said Kiki, proudly puffing out her chest.

"Being able to fly isn't always easy, huh?"

"Yeah, although not being able to fly must be hard, too," Kiki said, finally smiling at him.

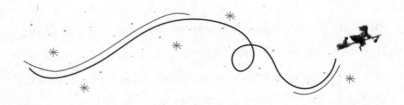

KIKI GETS
A LITTLE IRRITATED

The day after the horrible event at the beach, Kiki went to the western forest to find an ash branch for her new broom. She was no longer interested in a broom with a slender, elegant handle like the one she'd made before. She needed a type of wood that would be flexible enough to fly through the strongest winds, like a fish in water, yet have a sturdy core. After wavering for a while, she decided to attach the brush from her mother's broken broom to a new handle.

"Now it's half Mom's and half mine," she said to herself with a shrug. At first, she considered making an entirely new broom. But her mother's brush comforted her so much that she couldn't throw it away.

"Yeah, half and half is best," she spoke to herself again. Jiji was sitting next to her with his eyes closed, but when he heard her whispers, he peeked at the broom and sighed in relief.

The only problem was that the broom she made didn't fly very well. Perhaps the branch hadn't dried enough, especially since she had been in such a hurry making it? Or maybe it just wasn't used to flying yet? *Either way, I've got to master it on my own.*

Every time she rode it, she ended up dizzy, but Kiki didn't give up. The issue was that her mother's brush was more energetic than the handle, so the rear end kept bucking like a horse. When that happened, she'd nearly fall off the stick or suddenly flip upside down.

Whenever Kiki was flying around in such odd positions, far more townspeople called out to her.

"Miss! Are you all right?"

"Did you catch a cold or something?"

"If you're going to fall, do it right!"

Strangely, other people seemed to prefer her new flying patterns, saying, "I feel more relaxed now. When I used to see you flying through the air like a pointy black streak, you looked like a wicked witch from a fairy tale."

Kiki thought, *How can people like me more when I'm worse at flying? I guess Mom didn't realize* that *was a thing.*

About ten days after all the broom fuss, the 1-800-KIKI-CAN phone rang. When Kiki picked up, the voice of the artist who had painted Kiki and Jiji burst from the receiver.

"It's been so long! How are you? I finally finished your portrait. Come have a look, and afterward, would you mind delivering it to the exhibition venue? I heard you started doing that sort of work. As you know, it's a bit large, but I hope you'll find some way or another."

"Yes, of course . . . ," Kiki started to say. It would be very tricky to carry something so big yet flat like a board. If the wind was blowing, it would be even harder—and wasn't she already having broom trouble?

Years earlier, not long after Kiki had learned to fly, she'd delivered an umbrella to her father in a sudden rain. She remembered how scared she felt when a gust of wind popped the umbrella open and her broom spun like a pinwheel.

"It's a painting of you, so I'm extra pleased to have you deliver it." The artist seemed certain that Kiki would take the job.

"Okay, then, I'll figure something out," Kiki answered, without a choice.

"Great, now the request is official! Come pick it up tomorrow around noon. I'm excited to show the painting to you, too."

The next morning, there wasn't so much as a wisp of cloud in the blue sky. Still, Kiki was worried. A clear sky like this in the morning meant that the winds up high were blowing hard. And by noon, those winds sometimes came lower.

I wonder if I'll be able to carry it all right. It's an important painting. . . .

Just then, Kiki remembered the boy from the Aviation Club. He specifically mentioned he'd "studied a lot about how to fly smoothly."

She went straight over to Osono's to borrow the telephone book, looked up the Aviation Club number, and gave them a call.

"Is the boy—uh—the tall, skinny boy from the witches' broom research group there?"

"Skinny? I dunno what to tell ya. We're all pretty skinny."

"Oh, well . . . is there someone with scrapes on his forehead? I mean, if he still has them, I guess—"

"Ha—that one! He does, he does. He's definitely still scraped up. His name's Tombo. We always say his glasses make him look like a dragonfly. Oh, here he is—hold on."

A different voice came on the line. "Hello? This is Tombo."

"Oh, this is the witch from the other day. My name's Kiki."

"Wow, you found our number! Listen, I'm really sorry about what happened. Did I screw up again or something?"

"No, that's all over with. Today there's something I was hoping you could help me with." Then Kiki asked the best way to carry a large painting in the wind.

"You should put it on a leash. I think that's your best bet," Tombo answered right away.

"What do you mean?"

"Leave it to me. I think I can help."

"Gosh, thanks. The artist's house is on the edge of the forest in the northern park, practically buried in trees. Do you know which one I'm talking about? I'm headed over there right now."

"I know the place. It's like a badger's den."

"R-right. Well, see you there." *It really does look like a badger's den,* she thought. Kiki hung up laughing, then rushed around and prepared to leave.

When Kiki and Jiji landed at the edge of the park, Tombo came running up to them with a big paper bag.

When the artist saw Kiki, she cheerily brought the painting out of the back room.

"Oh!" Kiki exclaimed, and Jiji purred at the same time. The two of them gazed at a picture of a witch in a black dress and her cat against a dark sky. The black was so radiant and beautiful, Kiki looked down at her dress to check whether it was truly that stunning.

"Her eyes aren't quite right." Tombo had been quiet, but now he chimed in to complain.

"What's wrong with them?" the painter asked, surprised because she hadn't even noticed him yet.

"What do you mean, what's wrong? Kiki's eyes are much rounder, and prettier—"

"Ah, I suppose I could have painted them like that. But I was trying to bring out her witchiness." The artist observed Tombo with confusion on her face.

"Oh, this is my friend Tombo," Kiki hurriedly introduced him. "He came up with a plan to help me carry the painting smoothly."

Tombo didn't add anything. He just pursed his lips,

took another look at the painting, and got to work. First, he took a bunch of different-colored balloons out of his bag.

"Balloons? Are you going to use those to send it flying?" the artist asked nervously, holding the painting down.

"No, we're going to give it a leash," Tombo said.

Still unsmiling, Tombo took a canister out of the bag. He blew up balloon after balloon and attached long strings to them. Then he screwed a bolt into the frame of the painting and attached the balloons. Lastly, he tied a thicker string over the knots. The balloons rose into the air, and the painting hung just above the ground. It didn't float away, and it didn't sink—it hovered in perfect balance.

"The trick is to get the amount of helium gas and the number of balloons right," said Tombo, looking a little proud of himself. "Kiki, as you fly, hold this thicker string like you're walking a dog. If the wind tries to blow the picture away, pull on the string. Show it you're in charge."

"Is he calling my picture a dog?" The artist looked at Kiki with concern.

But Kiki was staring at Tombo with admiration. She never would have thought of such a solution, and she was grateful that he'd come up with it so easily.

"I think this'll work," Kiki said. "The painting will be a lot lighter this way, and no matter which direction the wind blows, it can move with it. This is a great idea."

When Kiki praised him, Tombo finally smiled, flashing his white teeth.

And it really *was* a great idea. When Kiki took off holding the string, the painting obediently followed. And when it twisted in the wind, she would simply slow her pace. Even before she reached the museum, people in the streets, looking out their windows, or tanning on their roofs saw the real Kiki and Jiji next to their portrait.

"It looks just like them," some murmured. "It's almost hard to tell which are real!"

One person even said, "It looks better than the real pair!"

In any case, the painting was very well received.

At the museum, spectators constantly crowded in front of the piece, which was titled *The Most Beautiful Black in the World*. Naturally, the artist was overjoyed. As a thank-you, she painted a striking picture of Kiki and Jiji on Kiki's shop sign. But more important, everyone all over the town of Koriko learned about Kiki and her business. In other words, she had managed to "advertise" just as Jiji had suggested.

From then on, Kiki was busier with work. She delivered flowers, forgotten lunch boxes, even soup to an elderly grandmother living alone. One time, she brought a doctor their forgotten stethoscope. Everyone learned that they could casually stop by and make their requests. But some people tried to take advantage of Kiki. They would make ridiculous demands like *Carry my backpack and come to school with me* or *Deliver this insult*. Of course, she always refused those jobs.

Eventually, the hot summer ended, and it started to look like fall.

Kiki had gotten the hang of her broom, and it

seemed she had finally settled into a good routine. But underneath it all, she was in a bit of a lousy mood. There was no real reason—she just felt irritated. *Everything's been so stressful since I got here. I'm just worn out,* she sometimes told herself. But deep down she knew that that wasn't it at all.

Ever since she delivered the artist's painting using Tombo's leash method, the boy had started coming around her shop. One day, he said something that she couldn't shake.

"Maybe it's because you fly, or something, Kiki, but you're so easy to hang out with. I can talk to you about anything. I've never met a girl in this town quite like you."

At the time, she took it as a compliment, but as the days went on, she couldn't get that last part out of her head. *I've never met a girl in this town quite like you.*

Back then he said my eyes were prettier than in the painting, and now he says he's never met someone in Koriko like me. Are girls from bigger towns different somehow? What does that even mean? She couldn't help but find that strange.

One day, one of her slippers was missing, and she took it out on Jiji. "This is so annoying! It's fine for you to play with them, but you need to put them back when you're done. How many times have we been through this? I don't have any matching slippers anymore."

Jiji yawned and pretended he couldn't hear her.

Then the phone rang. Kiki hopped across the room on her single slipper and picked up.

A calm voice came over the line. "Is this the witch shop? Good day to you."

"Uh-huh, sure," Kiki said absentmindedly.

"Can we really request *anything*? There's something I'd like you to deliver."

"Uh-huh."

"It's these biscuits. My elder sister, her name is Chrysanthemum. But my name is Violet. It's a bit embarrassing to have such a childish name as an old lady, ha!"

Although she knew it might be rude, Kiki cleared her throat. The lady was taking a while to get to the point.

"You'll go to my sister's house later," the woman continued. "First, do you know Goat Road? I'm at the end of it, nine-nine. Ninety-nine. Do you understand?"

"Yes, I understand. I'll be right over." Kiki didn't

even wait for her to finish before answering quickly and hanging up. Then she irritably kicked the slipper off her foot into a corner of the room.

Kiki found 99 Goat Road easily. When she pulled the string hanging beside the door, there was a soft rattling noise, and a voice from behind the house called, "Over here, please!"

Kiki walked through the alley along the wall and came to an open wooden gate. In the garden, an old woman with her sleeves rolled up to the elbows was doing laundry.

There were four big tubs in a row: one for whites, one for blacks, one for blues, and one for reds. Soap bubbles sparkled in the sunlight, floating around as if they were alive. The white tub had white bubbles, the black tub had black bubbles, the blue tub had blue bubbles, and the red tub had red bubbles.

"Are you Violet?" Kiki asked as she passed through the gate.

Without pausing her washing, the woman nodded. Her hair was cut short in a bob and scattered with gray. Beads of sweat stood out on her forehead.

"I'm from Kiki's Delivery Service."

Violet quickly wiped her hands on her apron and looked up at Kiki. "Not the witch shop?"

"Well, I deliver things."

"I heard you were a witch. I thought you took on any kind of job. But if you did any job, then you might steal my business, too! Anyway, I'm glad you only make deliveries. My business is a bit rare, you see." The woman let out a loud laugh. "Ha, I'm a handy-woman. It's similar to your job. Or maybe it's not?" Violet giggled at her own comment. "But I'm happy you're here."

She plunged her hands back into a tub and continued her washing. "My sister is so inflexible. If I say I'll bring something over today, it absolutely must be today or she'll get upset. Just a second, I'm going to wash this—*scrub-a-dub*," she sang to liven up the task of rubbing soap on a white shirt. "Delivering every little thing is a pain, so really, I'd like to live with her. But she says it's easier to live on her own. Okay, *scrub-a-dub, whap-a-dap*. Yet she can't bake a single biscuit!

"*Scrub-a-dub*. At least once a week I have to take something over there, or there's something to talk to her about. We're each other's only siblings. *Heave-ho, scrub-a-dub, whap-a-dap.* This spot just isn't coming out. Once more, then—*scrub-a-dub.* Can you believe it? But today I'm so busy, I don't have time. . . ." Still washing, she looked up at Kiki. "Sorry, I don't mean to keep you waiting. The weather was bad until yesterday, and I've never had this much laundry pile up in my life! I'm getting complaints from customers. I have to dry these as soon as possible—*scrub-a-dub, whap-a-dap.*"

"You're washing all of this?" Kiki's eyes widened.

"Yep. Isn't that obvious?"

"By hand?"

"That's right. I don't have a washing machine. But I take on odd jobs to help people make do, so I have to make do with my hands, too." As she talked, they continued their mechanical motions.

Kiki watched Violet's quick, skillful work in wonder. She stretched an item along the washboard, ran the soap over it, then rubbed it—*scrub-a-dub*—against the board. Then she spread the fabric back out—*whap-a-dap*—to check if it was clean.

She sang quietly along to her motions. *"Scrub-a-dub and whap-a-dap. Scrub-a-dub and whap-a-dap,"*

Bubbles floated continuously up into the sky. In no time, the whites, the blacks, the blues, and the reds had all been washed. Then she drew more water from the hose to rinse everything with the same *scrub-a-dub, whap-a-dap* motions.

Kiki watched in a trance, completely forgetting that she was there to work. Finally, all the clothes had been wrung out and stacked as a mountain of twisted bars in a basket. The whites were on the bottom, then the blacks, then the blues and reds. Violet straightened up, put a hand to her back, and looked at the sky with a deep breath. "Phew! Guess it's time to dry them."

She brought out some twine and stood there thinking for a moment, holding the end. Then she turned to Kiki, who stood next to her carrying Jiji and her broom. "Sorry, but could you hold the end of this for me? I'm going to hang the laundry. There's a lot, so I need a long line." Violet handed Kiki the twine without waiting for an answer. Then she picked a red ribbon off the mountain of laundry and hung it up. "We start with the littlest things," she said, again in her singsong voice, and speedily hung baby socks, a baby skirt, a woman's blouse, and more. With each item,

Kiki moved a little farther away. The line grew heavy and began to sag.

"It's going to touch the ground!" Kiki shouted.

"Oh, dear. Can you stand on your tiptoes, then?" Violet shouted back as she hung up a big red tablecloth.

"Agh, this isn't working! It's going to touch!" Kiki held the twine above her head and hopped.

"Hold it higher. Or perhaps you could use your broom and fly with it?" Violet said, looking up.

"Oh, that could work," Kiki said without thinking. Then she mounted her broom and flew as high as the eaves of the house.

Violet leaned back over the basket. Next were the blues.

"We start with the littlest things."

A mother's handkerchief, a boy's cap, a father's underwear, a girl's swimsuit, a father's shirt, curtains, and light blue sheets lined up all in a row.

The line threatened to touch the ground again, so Kiki flew as high as the top of the roof. Violet hung item after item, working up a sweat hanging.

Then came the blacks. A father's socks, a boy's pants, a mother's skirt, and a grandmother's dress lined up all in a row.

Then came the whites. A baby's mittens, a bib, underwear, and clothing—more and more, bigger and bigger. A mother's slip, a father's shorts, and finally five shirts.

"Ah, that's it!" Violet seemed relieved to be done, and she tied her end of the line to the fence.

"What should I do with thiiiiis?" Kiki yelled from far above the rooftops, waving her end of the line.

"Oh dear, what'll we do?" When Violet looked up, she threw her hands over her head in surprise. "Sorry! You can tie it any old place!"

"But . . . ," Kiki shouted back. Up in the sky, there was obviously nowhere to tie the twine. But if she let go, the laundry would have to be done all over again. Kiki gave up with a shrug and pulled the line to tie it around her waist.

"Wow, it's like we have a big, long tail!" Jiji leaned over the broom's brush and looked at the long line of clothes that waved like flags.

"How pretty! They're like the flags at Field Day." Violet hopped around below and clapped her hands.

People walking past looked up in surprise. "A string of kites, a string of kites!" A bunch of kids gathered around, cheering.

"This is no joke!" Kiki tried to frown, but she couldn't fight the smile underneath.

"Well, I guess I have no choice but to hurry up and dry these." Kiki began to fly, leisurely circling far above Violet. Each time the wind gusted against her, her unpleasant feelings from earlier slipped further away. "*Scrub-a-dub* and *whap-a-dap!*" She tried singing the tune she had heard from Violet earlier. And when she did, the sounds of the laundry in the wind accompanied her. *Whap-a-dap, whap-a-flap, whap-a-dap, whap-a-flap!* The sun in the clear autumn sky quickly dried the laundry. Soon, the sounds changed from *whap-flap, whap-flap* to *flutter-flutter*.

"Thank youuuu!" Violet called from below. Then

she tugged the line. One by one, she removed the items. And as Violet went, Kiki gradually came down, too.

By the time the whites, blacks, blues, and reds made a fluffy mountain in the basket, Kiki finally reached the ground. Violet ran over to her.

"I can't believe they dried so fast. You were a huge help!"

"I wouldn't expect any less from a handywoman." Kiki said with a smile. "You sure gave me an odd job—as a laundry pole!"

Violet shrugged her shoulders. "Yes, that's right. This is how we make do. If we manage, then we're happy. If we don't, then we're not," she said in her singsong voice, and carried the basket of clean laundry into the house. When Kiki followed her inside, she found all sorts of curious things. For starters, the door was split in two, so one could open it for just their face or just their feet.

"The door broke, so I make do with two smaller doors," said Violet.

The string by the front door was connected to a bundle of walnuts, nails, and spoons. She pointed to it with a smile. "This is a homemade bell. When you pulled the string before, didn't it make a nice sound?"

As Kiki was admiring the bell, she noticed a single boot with tall, fluffy grass growing out of it.

"And this is a homemade vase. Cute, right?" Violet smiled and little wrinkles gathered around her eyes. "Oh my, here I am getting all pleased with myself, but I was going to have you take biscuits to my sister, wasn't I?"

With an embarrassed look on her face, she brought two bags out of the kitchen.

"My sister lives in Pointy Manor on Dead Tree Road. It's the pointiest building on the street. And yes, these are for you—a little thank-you. They're called Star Dust Biscuits. When I was baking them, I messed up and they came out too small, so I made do with an adorable name."

Kiki was happy to have them.

When Kiki arrived at Pointy Manor, Violet's sister, Chrysanthemum snapped, "How spoiled she is, having someone else deliver them instead of coming herself! I'll have to give her a piece of my mind." But Chrysanthemum's eyes were happy when she peered into the bag.

That night, if you were near Kiki's shop, you could hear voices singing over and over,

This is how a handywoman makes do
If we manage, then we're happy
If we don't, then we're not

Inside, you'd find Kiki and Jiji singing into the solo slipper—a homemade microphone of their own.

KIKI PRIES INTO
SOMEONE'S SECRETS

*K*nock-knock-knock.

Kiki hurried down from the second floor and opened the shop door to see a girl standing alone in the doorway. Dark brown curls gently framed her face, and she wore a pretty, pale pink sweater. Gleaming white boots went all the way up to the knees of her slender legs. The girl almost seemed to be floating, Kiki was so awestruck by her.

"W-welcome!" Kiki was excited and could hardly speak—this was the first time she had a customer around the same age as her.

When the girl saw Kiki, she inhaled sharply,

lowered her eyes, and stumbled over her words. "I, uh, umm—"

"Do you need something delivered?" Kiki said, having composed herself a bit.

"I heard that this shop can deliver anything. Are you the deliverywoman?" The girl's tense face smiled, and she cocked her head.

"Yes, and I do a thorough job. No need to worry."

"I see." The girl nodded, her dark eyes flashing, and she seemed to purposely, slowly bat her eyelashes. "I want you to deliver something for me, but it's a secret."

"A secret?" Kiki asked, furrowing her brow.

"Oh, it's nothing bad." The girl lifted her chin and looked down at Kiki. Then she leaned on the doorframe with one hand. A silver brooch sparkled at the collar of her sweater. "I want you to deliver a present—to a boy named Ai. It's his birthday today. He's turning fourteen. Cool, right?" The girl spoke so proudly, one would think she had come up with the idea of his birthday herself.

What's so cool? Kiki thought, confused. The girl continued.

"But I don't want him to know the present is from me."

"Why not?"

"Why not? Well, Ai and I have known each other since we were little. He still only thinks of me as a kid, even though I'm thirteen now."

"But you want to keep this a secret? I don't get it."

The girl looked up at Kiki and cracked a smile. "You don't understand how I feel?"

Kiki was even *more* confused. "Wait, this present isn't something weird, is it? Will a frog jump out when he opens it? I don't accept those kinds of prank jobs."

The girl laughed again, this time a little smugly. "I heard you were a witch, but you don't know anything, do you? Is that what *you'd* do if you had a crush on someone?"

"Excuse me?" Kiki said, glaring at the girl.

The girl pushed her hair back with a bored look on her face and reached into her pocket. "I used all my allowance to buy matching fountain pens for Ai and me—look," she said, showing off a silver pen in her hand. At the same time, she flipped the collar of her sweater to reveal an identical one stuck through it from the inside. What Kiki had thought was a silver brooch was the clip of a similar pen.

"Carrying matching items like this is the latest trend." The girl, haughtier now, squared her shoulders.

Kiki knew this girl was a customer, and she knew she should have simply said, *I see* and delivered the pen. But when she opened her mouth, something else entirely came out. "What do you mean, you'll match? This Ai guy won't even know you're the one who sent it!"

"Right," the girl replied. "He won't. But I will."

Kiki couldn't believe the girl managed to brush off such a rude comment like it was nothing. Not only that, the girl was hardly paying attention, looking off into the distance somewhere, spellbound.

"It's a great present," said Kiki, pursuing the topic further. "But why not give it to him yourself? That's not so hard."

"I'm too shy for that." The girl slowly batted her eyelashes again. It was as if she thought being *shy* was a good thing. Intimidated, Kiki suddenly felt her chest grow tight—she couldn't pinpoint it, but somehow this girl felt much more grown-up than her.

"Shy? That's weird," Kiki said.

"Oh, you don't understand how that feels yet?" The girl smiled faintly, as if pitying Kiki.

But Kiki wasn't about to let this girl get the better of her, so she shot back, "You must be nervous about what Ai will think, right? What if he finds this strange?"

"Oh, I'm not worried about that. I just want to keep it a secret. It's good to be a little mysterious."

Kiki took another good look at the girl. She was surprised someone could have so many complicated feelings hidden beneath a simple pink sweater. *Mysterious? Is that how I'm supposed to act? Maybe there's something wrong with me.*

Suddenly she remembered Tombo's comment again: *I've never met a girl in this town quite like you.*

The girl in front of her continued talking. "Besides, once Ai knows one half of something, he'll just have to find out the other. So I'm going to send him on a hunt."

"To find *you*—the sender of the present?"

"Exactly."

"But what if he doesn't go looking for you?"

"That won't happen. He'll definitely look." She seemed quite confident on that point.

"All right. I just have to deliver the pen?" Kiki had the feeling this conversation might go on forever, and she wanted to end it.

"Please. And this along with it." The girl fished

around in her pocket and took out a small yellow envelope.

"A letter?"

"It's actually a poem. I wrote it. Don't you know you're supposed to send a poem with a present to your crush?"

Kiki felt as though the conversation was sliding backward, so she hurriedly asked, "What's Ai's address?"

"He lives on Dogwood Road across the big river. It's three eighteen, west of the zoo. But in the afternoon, he's usually practicing tennis on his own in the park."

"And what about you?"

"My name's a secret. I live on the next street over from Dogwood, on Kaya."

"If you're that close, you could just go—"

"But . . ."

"I—I know. I get it." Kiki held her hands up in front of her.

"If you see me, pretend you don't know me. And oh, right. I need to pay you."

After hesitating a moment, Kiki said, "If you don't mind, I'd like to hear how things turn out. Tell me later." A slightly spiteful part of Kiki couldn't help but wonder whether Ai would bother to search for the girl at all.

"You mean whether Ai tries to find me? So nosy! But sure, I'll tell you," the girl said, still self-assured.

"Then I don't need anything else in return."

"Really? You're sure?"

"I mean . . . ," Kiki started to reply.

"Oh, you want to learn how to talk to boys? I get it, I get it." The girl nodded, as though she was older and more experienced. Instead of replying, Kiki wrinkled her nose and tried her best to suppress a scream.

Once the girl left, Kiki turned to look at herself in the mirror. She combed her hair, adjusted the collar of her dress, and twisted and turned to look at herself from every angle. Then she sat on her bed and muttered, "What do I do if Ai thinks *I'm* the girl?"

Jiji flopped over next to her with exhaustion. "This is all so silly. I can't go along with this," he said, and yawned.

"So you're not coming?"

Yet when Kiki put the pen and the letter in her pocket and patted it to be sure, Jiji rose sluggishly. Outside the shop, the two of them took off. Lately, the wind had grown colder, and today it whipped at their cheeks. From up in the sky, they could see that fall was in full swing. The town had lots of ginkgo trees, and their leaves had all turned yellow. Every now and then, a stray leaf would flutter into Kiki's path and stick to her chest.

"You're really taking your time today, huh?" Jiji called from behind her. "You're going in circles!"

"Oh, am I?" Kiki returned to herself with a start and looked below. In truth, she had been thinking about one thing this whole time: the girl's poem inside the envelope that was inside her pocket.

When Kiki was little, she had written one poem herself:

> *Shoes laugh tap-tap-tap.*
> *Hats laugh tip-tip-tip.*
> *I laugh tee-hee-hee.*

That was the only time she'd ever encountered poetry, but Kiki knew that whatever was written inside the envelope couldn't be nearly as childish. *What sort of thing do you write in a poem to a boy? That girl seems to know so much. . . . She must have written something lovely.* Kiki's heart raced as she imagined all sorts of things. The more she told herself she couldn't look, the more the thought of the envelope occupied her mind.

"Jiji, I want to rest for a minute. I'm going to land on the bank."

"We just took off!"

"But it's fall," Kiki answered, knowing that was hardly a reason. Still, she began her descent, soaring in a big arc like a bird. Eventually she touched down in a park that ran along the river. There was no one around, and the swings swayed on their own in the wind. Beyond them, the river flowed by with occasional whitecaps.

"Jiji, if you want to go play somewhere for a little while, you can." Kiki leaned her broom against a ginkgo tree shedding its yellow leaves, and then sat by the leaf-carpeted roots.

"It's okay, I'll stay here. I'm cold. Fall can be over with already."

"Oh, Jiji." Kiki smiled tightly. "Why don't you go take a walk? Look at all the green foxtails growing along the bank. I know you like those," she insisted.

"Are you saying I'm bothering you?" Jiji narrowed his eyes.

"Yes, that's what I'm saying," she said jokily, pushing her hair into place after the windy ride.

"You're hiding something, aren't you?"

"Fine, you're right." Kiki shrugged. "But it's not as if I'm going to break it, or lose it, or get it all dirty. It's just for a second. Just a peek!"

"What are you even talking about?" Jiji frowned and stared her down.

"Jiji, don't get mad. I *have* to see what she wrote in her poem. I know it's wrong, but I need to look. Besides, I think this counts as part of my coming-of-age studies as a witch!" Kiki watched, waiting for his reaction.

"I don't see why you need all the complicated explanations. Just read it. It's that pretentious pink sweater girl's right? This is all very educational for me, too, so read it aloud."

"Oh, Jiji." Kiki could hardly believe Jiji accepted her excuses so readily as she pulled the note out of her pocket. The picture of a bouquet of flowers on the front of the yellow envelope seemed to swell off the paper.

"I hope it's easy to open. . . ."

When she lifted the edge of the envelope, the glue

came unstuck with a dry pop. Inside, a piece of paper with the same flower pattern was folded in half. The poem was written in cute, curly letters. Kiki sat the letter in her lap and quietly began to read:

Happy birthday
I wish I could say
But for some reason, I shy away
Happy birthday
I want to look into your eyes as I tell you
But for some reason, I shy away
I want to give you a present
From my hands to yours
But for some reason, I shy away
My heart celebrates you
But still, I shy away

"She's really shying away a lot, huh? Like a scaredy-cat," Jiji said upon rereading the letter in Kiki's lap.

"I wonder if she really wrote it. It hardly seems like her—she was so confident." Kiki cocked her head. "Well, time to seal it back up and deliver it."

All it took was an instant. Kiki held the envelope with one hand, but just as she reached for the letter

with her other, a gust of wind blew across her lap and the piece of paper slipped through her fingers and into the air. Kiki raced after it, but every time she tried to catch the letter, it fluttered among the falling gingko leaves and whooshed on, teasing her.

"Your broom, your broom! Hurry and get on your broom!" Jiji shouted in a panic.

Kiki doubled back for it, but tripped on a root and went sprawling.

"Oh no!" Jiji screamed.

When Kiki stood up, she caught sight of the yellow paper washing away on the river.

"No!" Her voice carried after it, but her legs weren't fast enough. By the time she reached the riverbank, the rushing water had taken the paper out of sight. "What'll I do?" Kiki stood there, dumbfounded.

"This time it's not my fault." Jiji said from behind her.

"I guess this is punishment for peeking at someone's letter." Kiki's shoulders slumped. "All I can do is apologize."

"You could deliver the poem aloud instead." Jiji did his best to console her.

"No, I understand how important this letter was to her. I wouldn't want someone else *saying* it to the person."

"Then what if you wrote it on one of these leaves? I pretty much remember what it said."

"That's true, and it's anonymous, so . . ."

"It'll be fine," Jiji said with certainty.

"Umm, the first part was 'Happy birthday.' You're going to help me out, right, Jiji?"

Kiki looked around, picked up a big gingko leaf, and sat back down under the tree. Then she took the pen out of her pocket, removed the cap, and began to write.

"After the 'Happy . . .' part, it was 'I want to say it to you.'"

"Yeah, and then it was 'But recently, I shy away.'"

"Oh my goodness, it's not 'recently,' it's 'for some reason.' And then . . . 'I want to stare into your eyes.' And then shying away again."

"She's not very good at this, is she?" Jiji interjected. "She says the same thing over and over again."

"Really? I thought it was pretty good when we read it before. Anyway, the next thing was about the present."

"The pen, right?"

Kiki looked at the pen in her hand.

"This really is easy to write with. So something like 'matching presents, silver pens' and . . ."

Thinking, Jiji looked up at the sky and said to Kiki, "It didn't say 'silver' in there."

"But I already wrote it. It *is* silver, so it's fine. Next is 'From my hands to yours.' I liked that part, so I remember it pretty well. And then shying away again. Or *does* she shy away again? That many times?"

"No. I remember, it was, 'For some reason, it feels like hide-and-seek.'"

"Oh, you're right, Jiji! I remember the end clearly— it was 'My heart celebrates you, but I still play hide-

and-seek.' Phew, I'm glad we figured it out." Kiki sighed.

"Let me see," said Jiji, peeking at the leaf. "Nicely done." He smiled.

They read over the recovered poem:

> *Happy birthday*
> *I want to say*
> *But for some reason, I shy away*
> *Happy birthday*
> *I want to stare into your eyes*
> *But for some reason, I shy away*
> *Matching presents, silver pens*
> *From my hands to yours*
> *But for some reason, it feels like hide-and-seek*
> *My heart celebrates you*
> *But I still play hide-and-seek*

Kiki and Jiji took off. They crossed the big river and dodged around the tall buildings, and when they saw the crowd at the zoo, they began a slow descent. She fixed her eyes on the park that sat partway down Dogwood Road. On the withered grass, a lone boy was hitting a tennis ball against a wall.

"That's him." Kiki quickly angled the handle of

her broom down. "You're Ai, right?" Kiki asked, approaching him after landing in the corner of the park. "Happy birthday!"

"Huh? To me? Do I know you?" His dark eyes watched her curiously.

"You're fourteen now, right? The girl who sent me is a *secret admirer*. I'm just the messenger," she teased with a smile.

"A girl? Who?"

"Wouldn't you like to know! She lives in this town. And here's a present from her." Kiki took the pen and envelope out of her pocket.

"Cool, it's so shiny. Looks like a rocket." The boy lifted the pen up to eye level and turned it around a few times before hanging it over the edge of his collar and patting it.

"Wow, you really do match now!" Kiki reacted with a shout, pointing at the boy's collar.

"Is the name in the letter?" The boy started to open the envelope. With a sickening feeling, Kiki remembered the leaf inside.

"Hmm, who knows? Well, I'll be going now," she spouted before turning and hurriedly walking off.

"Hey!" the boy's voice called after her. "Who is it? Tell me!"

Kiki shook her head without turning around. "I promised I wouldn't!" she shouted back.

So I guess she was right—he does want to know.

In her head, Kiki could almost picture the girl's happy face.

Three days later, the secret admirer came rushing into Kiki's shop like a leaf on a gust of wind. Remembering she had lost the letter, Kiki hung her head instinctively, but the girl asked in a singsong voice, "Miss Witch?" She sweetly twisted one of her feet back and forth. Her white boots gleamed.

"Ai found me. He asked if the present was from me."

"Oh, good," Kiki answered cheerfully.

"But something was weird. He also told me I 'really put some thought into that leaf' and said it was a great idea. Isn't that odd? Did a leaf somehow get in there when you were flying? I guess it doesn't matter. He knew it was from me because of the pen, not the leaf. You know, because I have the same one." The girl pointed to her collar and grinned.

Seeing how happy she was, all of Kiki's tension

melted away as if it had never existed. Feeling lighter, she braced herself and said, "To tell the truth . . ."

And at the same time, the girl said, "I have a confession to make. . . ."

"Huh?"

They looked at each other.

"You go first, Miss Witch," the girl said.

"I did something horrible." Kiki looked down and told the girl how she'd read the letter, how it blew away, and how she wrote the poem on a leaf and delivered it to Ai.

"Wow," the girl said, a bit disappointed.

"I'm sorry. But I think I remembered the poem right. When you came into the shop, you seemed to know everything. I really wanted to know what kind of poem you would write—so I couldn't help myself. I hope you can forgive me?"

"What, you thought that about *me*? I felt the same way about you," the girl said. "I didn't really think Ai would come looking for me. If I told him my name, I thought he wouldn't even care. But when I came here, you were so confident and seemed so much smarter than me, even though we're the same age. So I was determined to prove myself. I'm sorry. I think we have more in common than I first thought, Miss Witch. I bet we would get along." The girl smiled, batting her eyelashes as before.

Kiki smiled back at her and said in mock seriousness, "I may be a witch, but you can call me Kiki."

The girl giggled, then dropped her voice to mimic Kiki and said, "I'm a normal girl, but I suppose my name is no longer a secret—you can call me Mimi."

KIKI SOLVES
THE CAPTAIN'S PROBLEM

Fall was more than halfway through, and cold winds continued to blow every day. The withered brown trees lining the streets had long lost all their leaves, and the dried-up town of Koriko gleamed clear and bright outside the window of Kiki's shop.

As the wind blew between the concrete buildings, it cut sharp like a knife, then stopped suddenly before whipping up again. And with each gust, Kiki's humbly constructed shop creaked and shook.

I wonder if they already had their first snow back home. . . .

Listening to the wind, Kiki remembered what the beginning of winter was like in her hometown. One day it would suddenly grow cold, and when you looked out the window, the mountains beyond the northern forest would be obscured behind white as if a lace handkerchief had been draped over them. That whiteness would come down, down, closer and closer, until it covered the entire town. Back home, the sign of winter was the white of the snow, not the sound of the wind.

On the first winter day after Kiki had learned to fly, Kokiri took her out and said, "Everywhere you look is white, right?" She continued, explaining the dangers of the snow-covered roofs around town. "Sometimes the sun's reflection is so dazzling it hurts your eyes, so be careful when you're flying. What might look like a bean cake could be the roof of the fire watchtower. And what appears to be a staircase might be the roof of the library. That rectangular shape over there is actually the roof of the gymnasium."

"Witches are supposedly pretty tough against chilly weather, but the cold in this town seems to go right through me," Kiki murmured, pulling her collar up as she sat at the front of her shop.

"It's because you don't have anything to do. You're not moving around." Jiji teased as he jumped into her lap and curled up.

Kiki *did* have noticeably less work. Perhaps people didn't pay as much attention to details when it was cold, or they tried to avoid doing anything that wasn't absolutely necessary?

At times like this, I just want to wrap up in a blanket, drink something warm—like saffron tea—and talk with Mom. Remembering the relaxing smell of the yellow drink, she missed her mother.

"I wonder when's the best time to plant saffron," Kiki murmured to no one in particular. She regretted not learning how to grow the herbs Kokiri made every year.

For the hot pepper compress, do you boil them or sauté? She always used to tell me that there's something you can put in a soup when your stomach hurts. What was that? Kiki tried to recall things her mother used to do, but she couldn't remember the details. *Why was I so annoyed by everything she said?* Kiki frowned and lowered her eyes.

Suddenly she felt a gust of wind. When she looked, the door had opened a crack and four eyes peeked in. Then came a whisper.

"I heard that when a witch's cat gets cold, their eyes shine like a blue-green flashlight, but that's a lie. They're not different from any other cat's!"

"Where? Let me see. Oh, you're right. Then maybe it breathes fire? The older boy next door said you can use a witch's cat instead of matches."

Jiji knowingly exchanged a glance with Kiki, then turned toward the cracked door, widened his eyes, opened his mouth as big as he could, and exhaled, "Hahhhhh!"

"Whoa!" someone yelped, and the door slammed shut.

Kiki and Jiji listened to the nervous voices outside the shop.

"Did you see that?"

"Yeah, but you couldn't use it instead of a match."

"Or a flashlight."

"His eyes didn't shine at all."

"Yeah, he's just a normal black cat."

Little footsteps pattered away.

"Well, excuse me for being a regular old cat," Jiji grumbled. "Ugh, it's so annoying having these neighborhood kids peeking in all the time." He curled up in Kiki's lap again.

"Must be tough being so popular," Kiki teased. "What if you went along with it and dressed up strangely? You could dye your paws red or wear sunglasses or something?"

Jiji shot her a reproachful glance and then made up his mind to ignore her altogether.

A little while later, the phone rang.

"Oh!" Kiki exclaimed. "Maybe it's a job? It's been a while." When Kiki answered, a voice spoke slowly.

"Is . . . this . . . Kiki's . . . Delivery . . . Service? Well . . . I . . . have . . . a request. . . . I'm . . . an old lady . . . Oh, one . . . moment . . . I was holding . . . the phone . . . with my head . . . against my shoulder . . . and it almost . . . fell. . . . Both hands . . . are full . . . because I'm . . . busy . . . knitting. . . . I'm . . . an old lady. . . . The address is . . . two twenty-four . . . Silverberry . . . Street. . . . Please . . . come."

"All . . . right . . . I . . . will." Kiki started talking slowly herself!

Kiki and Jiji flew over right away, and when they got there, 224 Silverberry turned out to be on a smaller stream that branched off from the big river. The little house had a little pier painted sky-blue. When they went inside, they found that the old woman was little, too. She sat on a chair knitting.

"Oh . . . please . . . wait . . . a moment. This . . . belly band . . . will be done . . . in a jiffy." She spoke slowly and her mouth seemed to move in sync with her knitting needles. "I said . . . I could make it . . . in no time . . . but then my son . . . went and said . . . 'I don't need . . . that stupid . . . thing.' He's . . . still in his . . . rebellious . . . phase. . . . Oh, it's . . . finally . . . done."

Once she'd snipped the yarn with her scissors, she rotated her neck and shoulders. "Ahh, I'm pooped." Then she looked Kiki in the eye and suddenly spoke at a normal speed. "By the way, Miss Delivery Girl, how's your stomach?"

"Oh, I just ate, so I'm not hungry." Kiki bounced on her toes to show she had energy.

"No," the old woman said. "I'm asking if it hurts."

"Not at all. I'm in great shape. I can fly anywhere, no matter how far."

"It's when you feel that good that you have to be

the most careful. Don't let your stomach get cold. It's best to always keep it warm. Take very good care of it—your stomach is the center of the universe. And for keeping your stomach warm, nothing can beat a belly band. The best way to knit a belly band is using all different colors of leftover yarn and tying lots of knots. They're so warm, right? Don't you think?" The woman nodded in satisfaction without waiting for Kiki's reply, and then looked at Jiji, who sat at Kiki's feet. "Oh, and what about you?"

Jiji answered with a rumbling noise in the back of his throat.

"Oh no! That sound is proof your stomach's chilly. I wonder if I have a belly band somewhere around here that will fit you."

The old lady looked around. Surprisingly, every object in the house was wearing a woolen belly band: the phone, the coffee cups, the pots, the medicine bottles, the kettle, the thermos, the tea caddy, her boots, the potted plants, her walking stick. . . .

"Oh, yes. That one'll work." The woman stood up and removed the thermos's belly band. "A magic bottle that keeps soup hot and a magic cat—same thing. Plus, this belly band is a magic belly band, too—it has polka dots on one side and stripes on the other. It's perfect!" Her mouth wrinkled into a delighted smile as she put the band on Jiji.

The knit belly band was a mix of peach tones. The polka-dot side looked like apricot flowers in full bloom, and the striped side was like spring mist at sunrise.

"Oh, how pretty!" Kiki exclaimed. Then she said to Jiji, "It looks great against your black fur."

But Jiji didn't seem to care for it. He stuck his tail up straight, turned his head in a huff, and walked away.

"I'll knit one for you, too," the woman said somewhat apologetically. "It's not much for a delivery, but it would help me out if you'll accept two belly bands."

"Yes, of course. That's fine." Kiki smiled with a nod.

The woman smiled, too, and said, "You won't have to worry once you have a belly band. There's no better, cheaper way to stay healthy. Just the other day, I recommended it to the mayor. 'You want people to think you're an upstanding citizen, right? Better hide your flaws with a belly band.' And did you know that all the animals at the zoo got stomachaches from chilly tummies? I even recommended they give them belly bands! But the zookeepers are like my son—they never listen to me. Still, I don't care what they say this year. I'm knitting a bunch and taking them over there." The old woman had beads of sweat on her little face.

"Oh, I see." Kiki pointed at the pretty belly band the lady had just finished knitting. "You must want me to deliver the elephant's belly band." It had blue and white stripes that looked like a mix of clouds and sky, and it struck her as awfully big.

"No, this is for my son. He's a putt-putt boat captain. And he left early this morning, saying he had something very special to ship. You know the Morimo Peninsula all the way at the edge of Koriko Bay? Over there. And the precious cargo, well, it's fancy wine in bottles so big you need both arms to carry them. And supposedly, if you don't take extra care when transporting them, the wine will go bad all at once—*ker-bam*. Do flavors really make sounds like 'ker-bam'? I've never heard one like that before."

The old woman twisted her lips in thought and then continued. "Morimo Peninsula has two mountains, right? I guess that's why they thought it would be less rocky over the water. But the sea has mountains called waves—and far more than two! I wonder if they'll be all right."

The old woman paused for a breath but didn't wait for Kiki to reply before starting up again. "This is where the request for you comes in. My son's boat is a white boat called *Tete*. Lately, she's gotten old, like me, and instead of saying *putt-putt*, like a normal boat, she steams and says *pukaaatt, pukaaaatt*, like she's yawning. And to make sure the mission goes well, I want to give my son this belly band. I told him, so he should know to look for you. Search for them along the big river. They should be easy to spot. If he would just listen to me, we wouldn't have to go through this, but . . ." She shrugged with a sigh.

Kiki accepted the giant belly band but cocked her head. *Just how big is this son of hers? His mom is so little. . . .*

Then the old woman said, "If my son starts complaining again, you go ahead and put the band on for him. If it's too big, you can pinch it together; if it's too small, you can stretch it out. Either way, it'll be fine."

Kiki was still a bit confused, but she smiled anyway. "Okay, understood."

She slung the huge belly band over her shoulders like a cape and took off.

"This is so warm," Kiki said, flying with the belly band around her. "It's a great idea."

Jiji mumbled, "I've got a respectable coat of fur. If you put wool over it, I end up a sheep cat. But you can't say no to your elders."

Still, the peachy colors of his small belly band were pretty, so he didn't seem that upset.

"It looks good on you," Kiki said.

"Maybe this can count as dressing up strangely as you suggested," he said, reaching back to her earlier teasing.

Where the big river met the sea, there was a bay. Two large passenger ships were at the wharf, and another was being pushed in to anchor by a tugboat. Countless smaller boats sailed around the area. *Wheet-wheet-wheet!* Kiki heard a whistle blow some sort of signal. Out ahead and to her left, the Morimo Peninsula extended in the shape of a woman's lips. From high up in the sky, everything seemed to be moving so slowly that Kiki grew impatient. She periodically stopped to hover and look for the boat named *Tete*. When she couldn't find it in the port, she went farther out to sea. The wind began to blow stronger, whipping up from below. The number of boats fell off suddenly, so there was only a sprinkling here and there. In the distance, she saw what looked like a putt-putt boat. When she got closer, she heard the yawn-like *pukaaatt, pukaaatt* coming out of the smokestack along with the steam. Though the paint on the boat's side was coming off, she could still make out the name *Tete*.

Kiki called down to them from the sky. "Ms. Tete! Mr. Captain! I have a delivery for you!"

The sailors on the deck, gently carrying a load of bottles, jerked their heads up.

"I'm from Kiki's Delivery Service. May I land?"

"Sure, go ahead." The captain poked his head out of the wheelhouse and waved. Then he abruptly lowered his voice. "But please land softly so as not to startle the cargo."

"Oh, I thought you were transporting wine, but it's some kind of creature?" Kiki lowered her voice and quietly touched down on the deck.

The gathering of sailors stared, startled to see a girl fly out of the sky. But Kiki was even more surprised. The only big stomach she had imagined was the captain's, but all the sailors on the ship had perfectly round, puffy bellies, too. Looking around, Kiki said, "Captain, I have a delivery from your mother. It's a toasty belly band."

"What?" the captain said, exasperated. "My mother is awfully stubborn."

The sailors exchanged glances, as if to say, *There's no stopping that old woman.*

"I think this is too big for your stomach, though." Kiki spread out the blue-and-white belly band, which looked even prettier out at sea. "You'll be swimming in it. She said to pinch it together, but even if I did that—"

"What a thing to say! It's not for me. This belly band goes around the boat's smokestack—because she started saying *pukaaatt, pukaaatt* even though she's a putt-putt boat. My mother thinks it started because the smokestack's belly caught a chill. That's why she says a belly band will solve it, but I can't keep up with her nonsense."

"It's for the smokestack?" Kiki looked up blankly at the stack. *Aha. In that case, the size makes sense.*

The captain scowled. "Mother won't rest until she's warmed every belly in the world. What am I supposed to do? Take a look at this. I actually listen to what she says, and here's what happens to me."

The captain labored to unbutton his nearly bursting coat, and underneath it were layers and layers of belly bands. Bright colors swirled around him.

"Us too. We can hardly move."

The sailors next to him lifted their coats to reveal their own swirling belly bands. What Kiki had thought were round bellies turned out to be *belly band* bellies. She leaned back and burst out laughing.

"Umm, Captain? Isn't this . . ." One of the sailors spoke up nervously. "You're the Kiki's Delivery Service that gets buzzed about in town, right?"

"That's me." Kiki nodded.

"Then maybe we should make a request. Rumor has it you deliver anything. Could you carry this whole boat? There aren't any pesky waves up in the sky."

"Excuse me? What?" Kiki couldn't believe her ears. "The whole boat? That's impossible. Why would you ask me to do that?"

"It's because of this cargo," the captain said. "It's fine wine, so it needs to be transported with care. We aren't going far, so I thought it would be fine to keep the bottles on the deck, but that was a mistake. They end up banging together, which will ruin the wine's flavor. I've got all my men trying to hold them steady as best they can, but it's a tough job."

Once he mentioned it, Kiki noticed that the bottles

on the deck were rattling against each other, creating little bubbles in the wine.

"What if you let them go instead?"

"Then they'd just roll all over the place. Do you think it'd be too hard to fly with the boat?"

Kiki's eyes roamed around the ship deck anxiously. The sign at her shop said she could deliver anything. It wouldn't do to break that promise. But no matter how much a boat yawned *pukaaatt, pukaaatt,* it was still a boat. She couldn't simply pick it up and carry it.

"Um, well, the idea is that the bottles can't bump into each other, right?" Kiki looked back and forth between the sailors' puffy stomachs and the bottles that were puffed up in the same way.

"Yes, yes, that's right. It seems simple, but on a boat it's hard."

"Then I might have an idea. We can solve two problems at once."

"Wh-what's your idea?" The captain and his sailors all leaned in.

"But you'll need to go against your mother's advice." Kiki eyed the captain.

"Let's have my mother look the other way." The captain grinned and shrugged.

"In that case," Kiki said, raising her voice. "What if you all took off your belly bands and put them around the bottles? Then you'll be able to move around better. Plus, the bottles won't bang together, and the wine won't go bad."

"Ohhh, I see." The captain began to take off his belly bands at once. He pulled them down around his feet, and his round stomach disappeared. The sailors weren't about to be left out, so they began removing theirs, too. In no time, there was a mountain of multicolored belly bands on the deck, and next to it, a group of slimmed-down sailors.

They carefully dressed each bottle in a belly band. Now the bottles were lined up on the deck with multicolored belly bands. The rattling noises ceased.

"Aha!" Everyone nodded, relieved.

"Well, I'll be going . . . ," Kiki began as she mounted her broom with Jiji. But then she turned and told the captain, "Oh, I almost forgot the smokestack belly band! You should follow at least some of your mom's advice. How about putting it on?"

"Hmm, I guess you're right," the captain said. He seemed reluctant but also a little bit relieved. The sailors nodded in agreement. Then they all worked together to put the blue-and-white belly band around the smokestack.

"Okay, *now* I'll be going." Kiki waved and took off, then turned her broom toward the town of Koriko. Behind her she could hear the sound of the boat, and maybe it was her imagination, but she thought it sounded less like *pukaaatt, pukaaatt* and more like *putt-putt.*

The next day, Kiki saw something surprising in the newspaper. An article said the entire crew of the *Tete* had caught tummy chills. Below that was another item.

A liquor shop on the Morimo Peninsula has begun selling bottles of wine with beautiful woolen wraps. Both the wine's flavor and the bottle's looks are worthy of attention. It is a bit expensive, though.

A week went by and Jiji hadn't taken off the belly band the old woman had given him. On the contrary, he flicked it with his tail to keep it clean. Kiki suspected it had something to do with a townsperson murmuring, "That witch's cat is different from normal cats. He must be keeping his magic warm."

And about another week later, Kiki received word from the old woman that her belly band was finished. When she went to pick it up, the woman gave her a belly band knit with so many colors it looked like the inside of a jar of hard candies. "You always wear black clothes," the woman said. "So at least enjoy a bright belly band."

But Kiki had one final request. "Ma'am, could you please teach me to knit? I want to learn different skills."

"Yes, that's no trouble at all." The old woman smiled at Kiki. "What do you want to knit?"

"Something for my mom and dad—"

"Belly bands—of course! That's a wonderful idea."

KIKI DELIVERS
THE NEW YEAR

It was New Year's Eve in Koriko. In another four hours, the current year would be over. Every house seemed ready—all the windows were shiny clean, and an orange-colored glow spilled out onto the street from people's homes.

Kiki's heart ached. Back home, New Year's Eve was always a time for her family to enjoy together. But this year it was just her and Jiji, and she couldn't return home to celebrate her coming of age until a full year had passed.

In Kiki's hometown, it was a New Year's Eve tradition to eat big meatballs simmered with tomatoes.

So, Kiki pulled herself together and got to work. She made meatballs as big as apples and simmered them with boiled tomatoes she had saved from the summer, remembering how her mother used to do it.

At home, everyone would eat and share their memories of the past year. When the clock struck midnight, they would hug the person next to them and say, *It was a good year for both of us, wasn't it?*

"Hey, Jiji," Kiki said, shaking salt and pepper over the pot. "This year it's just us two, but let's eat meatballs, and when the clock strikes midnight, let's do the usual New Year's greeting, okay?"

"Sure, that sounds fine. Even if the year ends like this, we'll be all right. Depending on your perspective, it was a pretty good one." Jiji reached out his front paws and stretched.

It's New Year's Eve, but something seems off, Kiki thought. She cocked her head as she tasted the sauce. The streets were noisier than usual. People seemed to be gathering outside. *But now's the time to be around the table at home, not out around town.*

"Hello?" Osono opened the door to the shop and came in carrying her daughter. The baby was much bigger now and was even able to kick her legs. "Listen, can you hear it?" Osono said in a singsong voice.

Kiki looked at Osono blankly for a moment. Perplexed, she asked, "Listen? To what?"

This time it was Osono who stared blankly at Kiki. "Ah! That's right!" She shook her head, realizing her mistake. "You don't know how this town celebrates New Year's, do you? I should have told you. Look, see that clock?" She pointed out the window at the hazy clock tower in the distance. "I don't know who built it, but that tall clock over by the town hall—if you look at it, wanting to know the time, it's usually hidden behind the clouds. And even if it isn't, it hurts to crane your neck, so no one really looks at it much. But it does serve an important purpose once a year—on New Year's Eve. That clock *only* rings on New Year's Eve and *only* at midnight. It chimes twelve times—*bong, bong*. And then the entire town runs. We start by the clock and do a big loop around town. In other words, we kick off the new year with a running start. We've had this important ritual every year since the clock tower was built. And at some point, since we're all trying to make sure we don't miss the bells, our New Year's greeting ended up being 'Listen, can you hear it?'"

"So, *that's* why the streets are so busy?" Kiki said, finally understanding.

"Yes, naturally. The early birds left their houses a long time ago and are already out mingling and waiting together."

"In that case, is it okay for me to run, too?" Kiki asked, leaning in.

"Of course. But no flying!"

"I would never cheat like that."

"My plan is to run alongside my husband with the baby on my back. You can come with us."

As soon as Osono left, Kiki lifted her skirt and began stretching her legs and stamping her feet. Even Jiji shook his legs out one at a time, warming up.

Two hours later, the young mayor of Koriko, finished with all his work for the year, sat at his desk, stretching. After being elected at the beginning of the year, everything had gone well. And "despite being so young," the townspeople held him in high esteem for his performance. On this night, the last of the year, he felt more enthusiastic than ever. He was determined to lead the way in the New Year's race and prove himself as even more reliable to the townspeople.

One, two, one, two, he lifted his hands above his head; *three, four, three, four,* he stamped his feet. Then he opened his window, looked down at the town, and shouted the New Year's greeting at the top of his lungs. "Listen, can you hear it?"

In that moment, he was so shocked he nearly slipped through the window. His office was on the very top of the town hall, so with the window open, he could usually hear the faint sound of the clock far above in its tower, even if it was cloudy or raining. But instead of the usual orderly ticking, it seemed to almost be yawning—*tick-tock, ick-ock, pick-pock.* The mayor leaned out the window and looked up at the clock in a panic. Then the clock offered a final *ck-ck-ck* and stopped. It was ten-thirty-six. There was only an hour and twenty-four minutes until the clock's once-a-year job at midnight.

The mayor leaped for the phone and called the clockmaker who had cared for the tower for generations. "The clock tower clock stopped! Please come quickly—and whatever you do, don't let the townspeople find out."

As soon the mayor hung up the phone, he headed across the street and raced up the inside of the tower. The clock had never failed since it was built.

It ensured that the New Year Race started on time every year, and it was something the townspeople could be proud of. *Of all the times the clock could break down,* the mayor thought, *it had to be during the year I was elected. . . . What if this ends up in the history books? What a disgrace!* The young mayor couldn't bear it.

Before long, the clockmaker climbed up the clock tower's 2,358 stairs carrying his big tool bag. His family had cared for this clock for five generations. Thanks to their hard work, it had never stopped once. But now the clockmaker wondered whether he had made a mistake during the pre–New Year's mainte-nance round last week. His heart began ticking as loudly as the clock did when it was in working order. Though pale in the face, he got straight to work on the repairs. He used a little mallet to tap on every screw and gear. Almost immediately, he was relieved. "Oh, I figured it out. The biggest gear is broken. This makes it an easy-peasy fix. We just need to swap out the gear. It'll only take three minutes."

"Really?" The mayor started stamping his feet—*one, two, one, two*—but then asked, "Will the time be adjusted as well?"

"Yes, once the new gear is in, it'll be fixed in the blink of an eye."

"And the bell will ring properly at midnight?"

"Of course." The clockmaker was bursting with confidence, his earlier worries gone. Humming a little tune, he looked into his bag—at which point his face went pale again, and his hands began to shake. "B-but . . . I don't have a spare . . . g-gear. . . ."

"Wh-what? Then hurry up and go get one!" The mayor went pale, too, and his voice quavered.

"B-but . . . I don't have one at the shop, either. I— I'd have to order it."

"Then h-hurry! Do it!"

"B-but . . . it takes fifty-three d-days."

The mayor staggered backward. He groaned painfully before finally speaking. "There's nowhere you can get one?"

"I—I heard that the town across three mountains to the west has a clock with the same type of gear. So if we borrowed that gear—"

"Borrowed?"

"Yes, you know, without telling anyone—"

"You mean we'd steal it?"

"Yes, but . . ."

"*But* what?"

"But we don't have a thief."

"What are you talking about? You'll do it!"

"What? Ah, a-all right. B-but the time . . . Well, maybe if I go in a police car with the siren on I'll make it—"

"You idiot. Are you really going to go steal something in a police car? Isn't there some other way?"

"Uhh, hmm, well, oh, yes! There is, there is! That service in this town everyone likes so much. . . ."

Ring-a-ling-a-ling, ring-a-ling-a-ling!

The phone in Kiki's shop sounded, interrupting her preparation for the race. When she picked up, she did a little bow and said, "Listen, can you hear it?"

The voice on the other end was shrill in her ears. "I'm not worried about listening or hearing right now! This is the mayor. I'm told you deliver things, but I wonder if you can pick things up as well?"

"There's no need to snap. My business is deliveries, so if I can take something from here to there, I can certainly bring something from there to here," Kiki replied in annoyance.

This time, the mayor spoke a bit more politely. "Oh? That'll be a big help. In that case, would you come as fast as you can to the top of the clock tower?"

Kiki grabbed Jiji and flew into the sky, grumbling. This was the one night she didn't want to be flying. She wanted to run on the ground with everyone else. When she looked below, masses of people were already waiting outside town hall for the clock to strike midnight.

"To leap straight into business," the mayor said hurriedly the moment she arrived, "the biggest gear in this clock is broken. Do you think you could go to the town across three mountains to the west and—and, well, swipe one? As soon as possible, if you please?"

"Swipe?" Kiki's eyes grew wide.

The mayor slumped his shoulders and said in a low voice, "In other words, I mean, to just borrow their gear in secret for a little while so the bell can ring at midnight—"

"You mean steal it?"

"Shhh, that's not a very nice way to put it. We only want to borrow it. We'll give it back after."

"If that's all, then couldn't we just ring the bell? The clock is so high up no one can see it very well, anyhow."

But the clockmaker replied regretfully, "It was

made so the bell won't ring unless the hands move to the twelve o'clock position, as troublesome as that is."

"Then what if you just clapped your hands to announce the midnight hour, Mayor?"

"That's no good." He shook his head firmly. "We can't simply change such a long-standing tradition. If we do that, who knows what could happen! People might twist their ankles or break out in hives! I'm begging—won't you please go? We're running out of time," the mayor said, his face blushing red and going pale in turn. Then he furrowed his eyebrows and practically sobbed as he looked at Kiki.

This guy . . . , thought Kiki, pursing her lips. The next moment, she flew off without a word.

When Kiki flew west of Koriko and over the three mountains in a neat row, she found a town whose lights looked like a diamond necklace laid along the valley.

"Hey, Kiki, are you sure this is a good idea?" Jiji asked, clinging to her back. "We're not going to get caught?"

"We don't know unless we try. Maybe if we explain the situation, they'll actually let us borrow it for a little while," Kiki replied, mostly to convince herself.

The town was tiny, so she spotted the clock tower right away. She landed on the top and crouched to avoid being spotted. Looking down, she was surprised to see a group of people waiting in the square below, just like in Koriko. On top of that, they all seemed to be watching the clock. Kiki quietly made her way down the roof and landed on the ground. The people were chatting excitedly, but while they did, they all stretched and bent the fingers of their right hand.

In this town, do they exercise their fingers instead of their legs?

Just then an older man next to her smiled and said in a singsong voice, "At midnight—don't forget!"

It sounded just like Koriko's New Year greeting, *Listen, can you hear it?*

"What is everyone gathered here for?" Kiki asked.

"What? You don't know? At midnight, we pinkie-promise to have a good new year. That's been the tradition in this town for ages." He held up his pinkie finger with a smile. "Get ready. It's almost time. And, oh, I see you're carrying a broom. Still working on your New Year cleaning? Better hurry!" he said, playfully pushing her shoulder.

Stumbling slightly, Kiki made her way through the crowd and told Jiji, "Let's go back."

"What about the gear?" Jiji looked up at her, anxious.

"Never mind that. Let's just go," she said bluntly.

"But we were only going to borrow it for a little while. You're not going to ask?"

"No, how could I?" Kiki said sadly. "If I borrowed the gear, this clock wouldn't strike twelve. Then the people of this town wouldn't be able to make their pinkie promises. What if everyone ends up fighting for the rest of the year because of me?"

"But Koriko is in trouble, too. What'll we do?"

"I'll try to think of something." Kiki took off from the shadows and zoomed into the sky.

When she returned to the clock tower in Koriko, the mayor and the clockmaker practically pounced on her.

"How'd it go?"

"Hurry, the gear!"

Kiki showed her empty hands. "I don't have it, but don't worry. I'll make it happen. You two go wait down below."

"But . . ." The pair just looked at her and didn't budge.

"I'm telling you, it'll be all right. I'm a witch. I can handle it," Kiki declared. After herding the men toward the stairs, she spread her arms and took a deep breath.

"Okay, Jiji," she said. "Help me out. Hold on tight and push me with all your strength." With that, she mounted her broom and flew off at a tremendous speed.

Kiki went to the edge of town, spun back around, and went hurtling toward the face of the clock, accelerating even more. Then, just as she was about to crash, she grabbed the big hand with both of hers and used her momentum to push it toward the top of the face. And in the blink of an eye, her one push made one hour and twenty-four minutes go by. The two hands met beautifully at twelve.

Bong, bong, bong . . .

The bell echoed throughout Koriko, and a cheer exploded from the front of the town hall. Then feet could be heard pounding the street as the race began.

Meanwhile, having let go of the clock's hand, Kiki was flung all the way to the outskirts of town. When she finally coaxed her broom to a stop and returned to the clock tower, she plunked down, exhausted. Her hair stood on end, and the contents of her brain felt as though they had shifted to one side. When she shook her head and looked below, everyone was running in good spirits. The people whirled and eddied, and it almost seemed as though the street was moving. At the front of the pack, sticking out with his extra springy gait, was the mayor.

"That was wild. I thought my tail was going to come off," said Jiji, stretching flat as a pressed flower.

"I thought my eyes and mouth would fly off and I'd end up a faceless monster!" With a sigh of relief, Kiki looked at her watch. Oops—it was still five minutes before twelve!

"Ha, ha, ha!" She cracked up and bent over with laughter. "I guess we were a tad too good at our job. But at least we weren't late, so it's fine, right?"

"How sneaky of you," Jiji said. He was looking around, upset, when suddenly he yelped, "Agh! It's gone! My belly band's missing!"

"It must have blown away. Well, if that's the worst thing that happens tonight, I think that's all right— isn't it?"

"No, it's not. I was taking good care of that thing. Without it, I go back to being a normal old black cat. Instead of give-and-take, all I'm getting for my hard work in this town is a huge loss."

Kiki consoled him. "But we delivered the new year. How many delivery services have done that? Only we could pull off something that spectacular. You think any old black cat could do it? C'mon! Cheer up, and let's run with everyone. We'll have to cheat a little, but we'll fly to catch up to Osono and her family and run with them. We'll have to look for Tombo and Mimi, too. Hurry, let's go!" She scooped Jiji up, and they took off on her broom.

After the new year started, strangers would see Kiki in the street and say *Nice work*. She assumed every-one was simply in a better mood since it was the beginning of the year, but one day Osono explained it to her.

"The clockmaker has been going around spreading the word about you—saying things like 'Kiki fixed the clock and made sure it struck at twelve,' and 'It's pretty handy to have a witch who can use magic like that in our town.' I'm proud, too, because I've thought that all along."

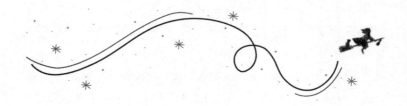

KIKI DELIVERS
THE SOUND OF SPRING

It was still cold every day.

Jiji was curled up on a chair complaining. "What a long winter. If it gets any colder, I think I'm going to quit being a cat. I can't take it."

"What would you be instead? You have such a nice fur coat." Kiki patted his back. "You keep saying you're cold, but the sound of the wind is already different. It sounds like spring now, I'm sure of it. Yes, spring—I'll be able to see Mom soon. But those who complain too much can't hear nice noises like that."

Jiji pouted and hid his face between his front

paws. But his cute black ears stuck straight up and twitched slightly.

Ring-a-ling-a-ling, ring-a-ling-a-ling, the phone rang. The moment Kiki picked up, a flustered voice came over the line.

"Umm, he-hello? Please hurry! Hurry! Come to the station, please—Koriko Central Station!" Abruptly, the call ended.

"Why is every job that comes my way such a crisis?" Kiki said.

When she arrived in the sky over the station, the stationmaster waved her down, shouting, "Here, over here! Hurry!" Next to him were eight men, thin like withered trees, in matching black outfits. When she landed her broom in front of them, they weren't surprised in the slightest. They simply continued glaring at the stationmaster with frightening looks on their faces.

"These gentlemen are musicians, and—" the stationmaster started to explain, but a man with flashing eyes cut him off.

"*Professional* musicians."

"Oh, right. These esteemed professionals will be performing this afternoon at the outdoor auditorium—"

"But it's so cold!" Kiki exclaimed. "Outdoor means *outside*, right?"

The man cleared his throat—"Ahem"—and puffed out his chest. "That's the whole point, because our music will warm your heart. It's called 'A Concert to Beckon Spring.' Well, it will depend on whether the ears of the people in your town are any good. But we're worried because we're missing something important."

"Y-yes, that's right. Miss, the thing is, the porters forgot to take their precious instruments off the train. It's quite a pickle."

The stationmaster removed his hat and used it to wipe the sweat off his forehead.

Nearby, Kiki noticed two young men, who must have been the porters, hanging their heads.

"Oh no!" She hopped up and down to look in the direction the train must have disappeared in.

"Yes, exactly. The train left with their instruments on board."

"Then please hurry and phone the next station. I'll go pick them up."

"The thing is, that train is an express, and after leaving here, it doesn't stop until the end of the line," the stationmaster said, even more upset.

"So what am I supposed to do?"

"Would it be impossible for you to take them from a window of the moving train? It's the car at the very end."

"Oh, there's no chance of that!" Kiki said, a little louder than she meant to.

"But it's been done before. One time, someone crept in through a window and stole a bundle of money."

"Well, isn't that awful! Why not borrow some instruments instead? We must have some in town."

"I thought of that, but—" The stationmaster looked at the men.

"That's unacceptable!" one of them yelled. "The mere idea is outrageous. We're not just *any* professional musicians. We can't make do with just *any* instruments. How could we perform with the kind of crude instruments that play if even a breeze so much as blows?"

The other seven men scowled even harder with their narrowed eyes and nodded in agreement.

"They have eyes as icy as the north wind, but they

say they're going to give a concert to beckon spring?" Kiki grumbled under her breath. "I'm not sure I like these guys."

"I feel bad for the north wind," Jiji murmured into her ear in a similar spirit.

"It's your fault for not removing them in the first place," one skinny man said. "We wrote 'To Koriko Station' on them clearly, so it wasn't our mistake. All the blame lies squarely on you, Mr. Stationmaster."

The stationmaster looked at Kiki as if she were his only hope. The porters were also watching her with desperation. She spread her arms and shrugged. If someone was counting on her, she couldn't say no.

"I don't know if I can do it or not, but I'll at least try catching up to the train."

"Hurry!" the man ordered her. "There's no time. We'll be waiting at the outdoor auditorium. Bring them by three o'clock. Got that?"

Kiki purposely flew off without a reply.

After quickly ascending, Kiki flew along the tracks. For a while, she soared through the northern part of town, but after she passed the fields and forests, the scenery became mountain after mountain and tunnel after tunnel.

"Hey, can you really pull off a stunt like this?" Jiji sounded concerned.

"Don't worry. Those guys were so arrogant, I just wanted to make them sweat."

"But we're talking about boarding a moving train!"

"It's okay. You're with me, Jiji. We'll figure it out."

"Huh?" Jiji shouted.

"Oh, there it is!" Kiki lifted herself off the broom for a moment and yelped. Ahead, the last car of the train slipped into a tunnel, like the tail of a lizard. "I've got this!" she shouted, and zoomed over the mountain to the tunnel's exit. "Jiji, he said it's the last car. So I'll land on the roof, and then you go in through an open window and unlock the back door for me."

Soon the train appeared with a *choo-choo*. Kiki angled her broom and prepared to descend.

"You're landing on that tiny spot?" Jiji sounded like he was going to cry.

Kiki didn't need him to tell her how tricky this would be; as she tried to aim for it, the train's roof looked like a flying leaf.

Agh, I'm a witch, and I don't even have a spell to make this train stop!

"There's no other way!" Kiki shook the jittery thoughts out of her head and began her descent. Wind whooshed past her ears, and both her hair and Jiji's tail stood straight up as if the sky were tugging at them.

"Ah! We're going to crash!" Jiji shrieked, but that was the moment Kiki went gliding down, body and broom, and clung to the roof. The train continued running as if nothing had happened. Kiki scooted along bit by bit, hanging on to the roof of the swaying car, and peered into a cracked window.

She spotted a mountain of luggage labeled TO KORIKO. *There they are.*

"Okay, Jiji, go in through here."

"I can't, I can't. I'll fall!" Jiji shrank back and clung to the broomstick.

"No, in you go." Kiki grabbed him by the scruff of his neck and shoved him through the opening in the window. Branches of the trees lining the tracks on the mountain whipped at Kiki's body. She flattened herself out to let them go by, but then came the next batch. "Hurry, Jiji! Open the door—please!" She stretched down and pounded on the back door.

Suddenly the train entered another tunnel, and everything went pitch-black. The wind gusted past her with a tremendous roar, and Kiki could feel herself slipping. In a panic, she grabbed her broom and tried to find a handhold, but just as she did, she slipped off the roof.

"Jiji! Jiji!" Just barely hanging on, she kicked the train car. At that moment, the door opened, and she tumbled inside. As the train exited the tunnel, bright light poured in through the windows.

Jiji sat on the floor as if his legs had given out from the fright. All he could do was stare at Kiki in shocked silence.

There was a whole mountain of bags in the car, but the eight instruments were in oddly shaped cases, so she could tell them apart from the other things right away. Even so, it was a lot of luggage.

"How are we going to carry all this?" Kiki plopped down like Jiji, exhausted.

"They have handles. Could you hang them from the broom?" Jiji said, seeming to have returned to himself as he sat next to her.

"There are eight of them, though. Do you think that'll really work?"

"Maybe not."

"Oh, wait a second. Maybe if we take them out of their cases, they'll be a little lighter."

Kiki opened the case nearest her. Inside was a shiny golden instrument shaped like a twisty slide at an amusement park.

"This one is a horn—you blow into it. Oh, here's a trumpet. And a trombone. This is a violin and here's . . . a cello! Dad taught me about all of these."

Kiki opened case after case. Each instrument sparkled, as to be expected, given how proud the musicians were of them.

"Jiji, you can carry a violin, right? I can carry the cello. Let's thread the brass section from biggest to smallest like a necklace and hang it from the broom. We can use bits of the string from those packages," Kiki explained busily as she began to connect the instruments. Then she tied them to her broom and said, "Okay, Jiji, time to go. Hop on the back."

Kiki straddled the broomstick, holding the cello against her lap with her right hand and the bow in her left. The violin was bigger than Jiji, but he held it with all four of his paws and sat with his tail wrapped around the broom's brush.

"And we're off. Let's go!" Kiki shouted, and flew out the open door. The brass instruments took off one by one behind her.

Pree, pree, pu-pu-pree!

As soon as the wind hit them, the horns began to make noises. Surprised by the sounds, the passengers of the train looked out the windows, pointing and yelping.

"Ha!" Kiki exclaimed, "You never know what can happen in the sky—and this is pretty special."

Riding the rush of confidence, Kiki began to play the cello in her lap. Jiji plucked the violin strings with his claws. It was the first time playing an instrument for them both, so the sounds were squeaky and screechy. It was bad enough to rattle the teeth of anyone listening. The brass instruments continued making bizarre sounds in the wind, like pigs or people snoring. But once the breeze from the south mixed in, it became fun and rhythmical. Kiki wove this way and that, climbed up and dove down, trying out all different sounds as she headed back to town.

Meanwhile, the outdoor auditorium in Koriko was full of people. It was already ten minutes past three, the time when the concert was supposed to have started. A poster reading A CONCERT TO BECKON SPRING hung at the center of the stage, and below it, the eight musicians sat in a row with their sharp features facing the audience. They may have looked composed, but inside they were terribly nervous about whether Kiki would manage to deliver their instruments or not. Most anxious of all were the stationmaster and the porters backstage.

"We're cold, so please start already!" someone from the audience shouted.

"We're going to freeze. Aren't you supposed to be beckoning spring?" someone else jeered, and everyone laughed.

One of the musicians stood and said, "The performance will begin momentarily. Please wait with open ears. Though it's cold outside, once we start to play and the beautiful sounds come forth, spring will warm the hearts of anyone listening. We're currently dedicating a prayer in preparation." The musician gazed out over the audience and then cleared his throat in a haughty way. "A-hrm-hrm."

The other musicians hid their irritation by clearing their own throats, then bowed their heads and pretended to pray. The audience thought disrupting them would be unkind, so they quieted down and bowed their heads as well.

Then came a faint, faint sound.

Fwahhh, fwah-wah, praaah.

Whaaa, whaa-whaa, hrarahh.

Yaaaa, yaa-yaa, yararahh.

From between the clouds, beyond the mountains, over the big river, and toward the sea came a sound like a whisper, an invitation, a secret—it was as if the prayer had worked and spring was on its way. The audience and musicians all looked up, one after the other. Something in the sky was catching the sun's light and shining brightly. It swung and swayed as it approached.

Fwahhh, fwah-wah, praaah.

Koo-ree-ree, koo-ree-ree!

Whaaa, whaa-whaa, hrarahh.

Poo-ree-ree, poo-ree-ree!

Yaaaa, yaa-yaa, yararahh.

The people huddling into the collars of their overcoats, the people curled up in balls, and the people hugging their knees—they all stretched out. It was as if the beautiful approaching sounds were pulling them closer to spring. But the musicians on the stage were shocked. They exchanged looks, blinking furiously, and whispered, "Who could be playing them?"

Soon the gleaming cluster in the sky was easier to see. Of course, it was Kiki on her broom with Jiji and the string of brass instruments like a necklace of light. The flustered musicians stood and disappeared backstage so they could receive their instruments the moment Kiki landed and begin the performance.

The stationmaster and the porters waved their hands with all their might to signal her. But Kiki pretended not to notice them. She was having too much fun playing the cello along to the brass noises.

She turned around and said to Jiji, "Let's fly a little more."

"Sure! Considering the train door might not have opened at all, I think they can wait a little longer." Jiji was holding the violin and seemed in no hurry, either.

Below, the audience whispered.

"Oh, I see! This is a wonderful concert."

"I never expected music to come raining out of the sky. . . ."

Some people simply closed their eyes in bliss as

they listened. Others waved at Kiki. Some moved their feet to the beat.

"I have to get ready for spring."

"Yes, this year I think I'll put violets in my hat."

Everyone was excited, as if spring had already arrived.

Before long, someone began to clap, and soon a huge round of applause echoed on and on.

"Okay," Kiki finally said, "I'm going to land."

She reeled in the brass instruments so they wouldn't hit the ground and get scuffed. Then she made a smooth landing backstage, where the stationmaster, the porters, and the musicians were waiting. When the audience could no longer see Kiki, they clapped even louder and offered a standing ovation.

Meanwhile, behind the stage, the musicians pounced on her impatiently.

"How slow!" they complained as they set about removing their instruments from the string.

"It was the wind's fault," Kiki said calmly.

The musicians grabbed their instruments and dashed out onto the stage. But the audience was already on their way to the exit.

"Excuse me," the musician called out, and one of the concertgoers turned around.

"Thank you for the delightful music," the concert-goer said. "It was a great idea to have that sweet witch deliver it from the sky. Please visit our town again!"

Hearing that, all eight of the musicians' jaws dropped.

Kiki and Jiji mounted the broom and flew off to return to the shop.

"Hey, Kiki, did you get anything as a thank-you?" Jiji asked.

"What are you talking about? I had so much fun! What could I possibly ask for after that?" she said, turning to him in surprise.

"Yeah, you're right." Jiji nodded and stuck his ears straight up. "I can still hear the sounds of spring."

"That's because those are the *real* sounds of spring." Kiki looked at the town of Koriko spread out below. "I've been here an entire year."

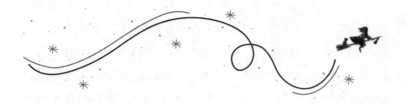

KIKI VISITS HOME

Spring was in full swing in Koriko.

Kiki pulled a chair over to the sunny window and sat, hugging her knees. When she looked up at the sky, it was vaguely hazy with sunlight as soft as a baby's cheeks.

"The day after tomorrow will be exactly a year. We can visit home." Kiki had been murmuring this to herself all day.

As the year-mark approached, she strangely felt both happy and nervous.

"Yep," Jiji said. "There're just two days left, today and tomorrow. There's nothing you need to get ready?"

"I mean, it doesn't have to be exactly a year."

Hearing that, Jiji paced restlessly, slapping his tail against the floor. "What's wrong, Kiki? You were looking forward to visiting so much! Now that the day's practically here, you're so indifferent about it."

Kiki stared at her knees, grabbed her skirt, and stretched her legs out at an angle with her toes in line. "Do you think I've changed? Do I seem older?"

"You're taller."

"Is that all?"

"I don't *know*." Jiji shook his whiskers in annoyance.

"Do you think I really came of age?" Kiki asked.

"What are you saying? It's been a year!" Jiji looked at her in surprise, but then cocked his head and consoled her instead. "I think you've done a fine job."

"Thanks," Kiki said quietly.

Kiki had followed in her mother's footsteps, as daughters often chose to do. She decided on her own to live in Koriko and even began her very own business, Kiki's Delivery Service. There had been many challenges, but she had done her best. Yet now she was unexpectedly anxious. *Have I really succeeded?* Before she came of age, she might have bragged to everyone, *Look at all I've done! Aren't you proud of me?*

But now she didn't feel very confident, even with Jiji telling her she did a "fine job." She needed someone else to confirm it was true.

"You're not saying you want to put off going home, are you?" Jiji gave her a sideways glance.

"Of course not." Kiki hopped up and gave her back a good stretch—that was enough mulling for now. "Okay, time for work. Visiting home is a job, too. Let's 'deliver' ourselves to Mom and Dad. Ready? Time . . . to . . . go!"

"Yay!" Jiji said lightheartedly as he did a backflip. Kiki was in a much better mood now and began bustling around.

"First, we need to let Osono know."

"Oh my, the day after tomorrow? I didn't realize it was so soon. How long are you planning to be gone?"

Osono had always known that Kiki would visit home at some point, so she wasn't very surprised.

"Hmm," Kiki thought. "Fifteen days or so? It's been a year, after all. I'd like to take it easy for a little bit."

Osono grinned and poked Kiki's cheek. "You're already starting to sound like your mama's little girl again. Usually when people say they'll be gone for a little while, they mean ten days, not fifteen. Make it a short while and come back soon."

Kiki blushed and stuck her tongue out.

After that, she called Tombo.

"I'm jealous," he said. "Sounds like a long trip. How fast will you fly? How high? With the wind, or against? What's the temperature up there? What's it like to fly through clouds? Do they have a flavor?"

The whole time they talked he only asked about flying. *Does he have nothing in his head besides questions? He's always like this, always studying.* When Kiki hung up, she couldn't help but feel dissatisfied and glared at the phone.

Next, she called her many regular customers, plus her friend Mimi, and once that was done, she made a sign with a notice on it: SORRY FOR THE DISRUPTION, BUT I'M GOING ON VACATION FOR A LITTLE WHILE. In the corner, she wrote, A LITTLE WHILE IS ABOUT TEN DAYS.

That night she told Jiji, "Tomorrow we'll clean the shop, and then the next day we'll leave early in the morning. That's fine, right?"

Jiji couldn't stop grinning. He ran in circles trying to catch his tail, then suddenly stopped when he remembered something. "What souvenirs should we bring for Kokiri and Okino? You have to get them a present."

"We have a ton of stories to tell them."

"Is that all? What about the belly bands? You were knitting them, weren't you? With blue yarn?"

Kiki silently furrowed her brow.

"You didn't finish them? Hmph, that's no surprise. You couldn't stick with making sneeze medicine, and you can't stick with this sort of work, either?" Jiji heaved a sigh at her feet.

"Well, that's not a very nice thing to say." Kiki cracked a smile, ready to share a secret. She took a puffy paper bag off the bookshelf. "I *did* stick with something, so there," she said, shaking out the contents of the bag. A little belly band, knit in a bright blue pattern scattered with gray, landed on the floor. "It's for you, Jiji. I made it so you can look fancy when we go home, since the one the old lady made for you blew away."

When she put it on Jiji, words failed him, so he ran happily in circles.

"And I made Mom's and Dad's, too." Kiki pulled out two belly bands featuring lots of orange and green. "It was hard to knit without you noticing."

"That's so sneaky! I can't believe you kept it a secret."

"But you know, a good secret makes things three times as nice."

"A good secret? Maybe that's not a bad idea. Okay, got it."

"You got what?" Kiki asked.

But Jiji just replied, "Nothing," and zoomed around in circles again.

The next day, while Kiki and Jiji were cleaning the shop, Tombo raced in panting. Then, with a face so red he looked angry, he thrust a paper package at her and said, "For you!"

Sometimes, I really don't understand boys, thought Kiki as she opened it. Inside was a little shoulder bag. A black cat was embroidered on the pink fabric.

"Aw, how cute!" Like Jiji the day before, more meaningful words failed Kiki, too.

"You like it?"

Kiki nodded.

"Oh, good," he replied bluntly. "Take it with you." When she slung it over her shoulder, he blushed and blurted, "Well, you're leaving tomorrow, right? Take care!" Then he gave Jiji a little tap on the head and rushed away just as fast as he had come.

Dazed, Kiki watched him go. "What's gotten into him?"

"It was pretty thoughtful of him to choose a black cat design." Jiji noted in Tombo's defense.

"That's true." Kiki nodded, filled with happiness. "If he picked this out for me, he must like me exactly the way I am."

When she undid the little bag's red button, she found a scrap of paper inside. "Oh!" she cried. The paper said, *I'll be waving from the bridge over the big river. Tombo.*

"What is it?" asked Jiji.

"Ah, it's nothing. Just . . ." Kiki shook her head, put the paper back inside, and patted the purse.

"Okay, we're off!" Kiki called to Jiji, turning instinctively to look back into her shop as she went outside with her broom and bags.

Her red phone, her desk made of boards and bricks, the map, the narrow staircase, the sacks of flour in the corner, all the little necessities she had bought since moving to the town—suddenly, they were all memories of the past year, and Kiki felt a twinge in her heart.

"Let's go," she said after taking a big breath, her voice a bit shaky.

When Kiki hung her sign on the door, Osono came out of the bakery with a large bag of bread, and her husband followed, carrying the baby.

"I have a job for you, Kiki," Osono joked. "Please deliver this bread to your mother. Don't forget to tell her it's from the best bakery in Koriko!" Osono noticed Kiki's saddened face and laughed loud enough to send those feelings out the window. "Kiki, make sure you come back, all right? We're so happy to have a witch as our neighbor. Everyone says that if they go three days without seeing you flying through the sky, they feel like something is missing."

Kiki thought she might cry. Her face twisted as she gave Osono a huge hug. "Of course! Of course I'm coming back."

Kiki soared high into the air with the souvenirs

tied to her swaying broomstick. Koriko was slightly hazy with the morning mist coming from the sea. After flying over town in a big circle around the clock tower, she slowed and flew toward the bridge on the big river.

Oh, there he is. Tombo sat on his bike in the middle of the bridge, waving both hands in huge arcs. Kiki waved back.

"Isn't that Tombo?" Jiji asked in surprise from behind her.

"Yeah," Kiki said proudly.

"Did you know he would be there?"

Kiki didn't answer and just kept waving.

"You're not going to land? Don't you feel bad just waving without a proper goodbye?"

"This is enough—it's fine." Kiki waved even harder, flew two laps of the bridge end to end, then snaked left and right before zooming off toward the north. Tombo grew smaller until he was hidden behind the bridge.

"Okay," she said. "We're on our way."

Now all she had to do was fly in a straight line home.

Her broom soared smoothly, flying no differently from Kokiri's old broom. When did her kicking filly learn to cruise so nicely? She marveled anew at the thought.

As Kiki flew, the bits of joy and wonder she had shared with the people of Koriko became clear. Osono had told her to *come back soon*. And Tombo had gifted her the purse—he must have felt the same way. Some townspeople even thought that something was missing if she wasn't flying through their sky! As she traveled on, her doubts and worries receded behind her with the wind.

Kiki and Jiji's journey went much faster than it had a year ago.

The sun set, the first star of the night shone faintly, and by the time the sky was dark and twinkling, a familiar town came into view at the edge of the forest. All the houses in their quiet rows had lights on. Unlike the seaside, the forest air seemed heavy with the nighttime dew. And the most comforting thing of all were the bells that still gleamed dully at the tops of the tall trees.

Kiki aimed directly for her house on the eastern end of town and stopped to hover over the roof.

"Oh, smells like bean soup!" said Jiji.

"Right? I had a feeling she would make that—since it's our favorite."

Kiki and Jiji took some deep breaths of the homey scent, and then they landed softly in the garden. They crept quietly over to the door and gently knocked.

"Come on in!" It was Kokiri's voice. "Sorry, my hands are full at the moment."

Kiki and Jiji looked at each other and nodded mischievously. Kiki cracked the door and said in a low, manly voice, "Hello? Delivery, ma'am!"

Kokiri whirled around to look from the kitchen, and Kiki pushed the door wide open.

"Oh, Kiki! It's you! I thought for sure you wouldn't be here until dawn at the earliest." She gestured to Kiki with a hand holding a dripping ladle.

"But it's just like you said, Mom! You were sure I would come home after exactly a year."

"That's right."

Kiki left her bags and the broom by the door and ran to her mother.

"Well, well, well," Kokiri repeated, putting her hands on Kiki's shoulders. And every time she said it, Kiki nodded.

Okino came out of the next room and stood back, watching the gleeful reunion with a smile. After a little while, he finally entered the conversation, joking, "I sure hope you didn't forget about me."

"Oh, Dad! I'm home!" Kiki threw her arms around his neck.

After the rush of happy squealing and fussing came the chatting. Kokiri said something, then Kiki, while Okino and Jiji simply watched in astonishment. Could that many words really fit inside the two of them?

Kiki brought out the bread from Osono and showed them the belly bands she had knitted.

"Wow, you learned how to do this? Amazing!" Kokiri put the belly band on beneath her clothes right away and patted her stomach.

"Mom, I'm pretty sure that lady puts her own mysterious powers into the belly bands when she knits them."

"Lots of older people seem to have powers like that," Okino said, looking at the belly band in his hand.

Just then, as if he had been waiting for the right time, Jiji stretched up and peeked out from the other side of the table. Then he gently dropped a light purple shell out of his mouth in front of Kokiri.

"Oh, you brought me a souvenir, too?" Kokiri asked in surprise.

"What? Jiji, you kept it a secret?" Kiki yelped, even more surprised.

He whispered in her ear, "I picked it up last summer when we went to the beach. A good secret makes things three times as nice, right?"

And it truly was three times as nice. Kokiri set it on her palm, turned it over and over, and leaned in for a closer look. "This is a shell, right? Is this the color of the sea?" she asked.

"Yes, it looks just like the color of the sea at dawn," Kiki answered.

Then Kokiri turned to look sentimentally at Kiki and Jiji and said, "You've both come so far. Just the other day you were babies, and now look at you, all grown up. . . ."

Hearing her mother say that, Kiki felt her heart quietly fill with pride. Kokiri answered the question Kiki had desperately wanted to ask. And it was then that Kiki realized: Kokiri was the person she wanted to ask most of all.

"Mom, I've been thinking that witches shouldn't *always* rely on their brooms. Of course, with my new business I'm usually delivering things in a hurry, so

I need to fly. But sometimes it's good to walk. When you walk, you end up talking to all sorts of different people even if you don't even want to, you know? I met Osono because I was walking. If I had flown to distract myself from how sad I was, who knows how I would have ended up? And when people see a witch up close, they realize that we don't all have pointy noses and gaping mouths. We can discuss things and maybe come to understand each other."

"Yes, you're exactly right." Kokiri nodded, impressed. Okino looked at Kiki with wonder-filled eyes, as if he was seeing his daughter for the first time.

Starting the next day, Kiki lived just as she did when she was a kid.

"Those old habits come right back, huh?" Kokiri laughed. "Well, that's fine. It's one year versus thirteen, after all."

Kiki drank tea out of her favorite teacup and primped to her heart's content in front of the mirror. At night, she slept hugging the same flower-patterned comforter she had been using since she was a baby. And every morning, she didn't wake up until her eyes opened naturally.

Whenever she had time, she walked around town. Everyone wanted to be the first to greet her.

"Oh, Kiki, you're back?"

"Oh, Kiki, look how pretty you've gotten!"

"Oh, Kiki, been a while. Come by for a chat!"

Kiki was so happy to have people who cared about her. *You really can't beat home.*

But after five days of this, Kiki found herself thinking about Koriko.

Osono's laughter, freshly baked bread, this neighbor and that neighbor who would talk to her through her open window, the tree-lined path along the big river, the smell of the sea, the tall clock tower, the smile of her friend Mimi—she missed every little thing. And Tombo. The sight of him on that bridge, waving for all he was worth, stayed in some corner of her heart, pulling her back to Koriko. She knew they would have lots to talk about the next time she saw him.

And what about her shop? The phone could be ringing right now! So many things were on her mind that even though she was home, she felt like she was just stopping by and couldn't quite relax. She had only lived in Koriko for a year—this longing to return was strange and unexpected, even for her.

Finally, she said, "I think I'm going to go back to Koriko, tomorrow or the day after."

"Oh? I thought you were staying for ten days."
Okino looked at her in surprise. "Is life here boring
now?" he asked.

"No, it's not that. But there might be customers
waiting for me. My phone might be ringing—"

"If you start to worry about things like that, there's
no end to it. When you're here, you're here."

"But . . ." She started to say something but stopped.
Kokiri and Okino had waited a whole year to see her.
Perhaps it wasn't fair of her to say she was leaving
early.

Then Kokiri, who had been silent next to her,
spoke. "It might be better for you to go back. When
I was young and traveled home from this town, I remember the bizarrely strong pull to return. If you
weren't anxious about what was going on in Koriko,
that would be its own problem. But, Kiki, please come
back next year."

The next day, Kiki and Jiji flew east to Mount Green.
Sitting on the slope overlooking the town, they took
in all they could see.

"Jiji, I've decided to go back. That's okay, right?"

He was teasing the bugs in the grass with his front paws. "Sure. Although you'll have to pack up right after you unpacked."

"I already thought about what to get for souvenirs."

"Are they secrets this time, too?"

"No. For Osono I'm bringing some of Mom's medicine. I think sneeze medicine will be great for the baby. I wasn't sure what to do for Tombo, but then I thought, what if I gave him one of the bells from the treetops—the ones Mom hung? If I took the biggest one and polished it up, I bet it would shine. And, it's a piece of my childhood."

"Yeah, that's a good idea. It's a thousand times more thoughtful than a fountain pen." Jiji nodded.

"Oh, Jiji!" Kiki laughed. "The bell has a pretty sound, so I'm not going to include a poem. I don't know what I would write, anyhow."

The smell of grass rose from the ground beneath her feet. The moos of cows, both high and low, drifted over on the soft breeze. When she lay down and closed her eyes, the light of the sun became green polka dots that moved around under her eyelids as if they were swimming.

How wonderful it is to have a place to return to.

Coming home, she had discovered a new version of herself.

When Kiki got back to the house, Kokiri chuckled and said, "Did you go to Mount Green?"

"You can tell?" Kiki asked.

"Yes, you still have very clear grass lines on your face!"

That afternoon, Kiki went with Kokiri and took down all the bells that hung from the town's trees.

"This past year, every time the wind rang these bells, I thought of you." Kokiri smiled tearfully, her feelings complicated.

"It's sad to think I don't need them anymore," Kiki murmured.

Kokiri replied, "I'll put them away and take good care of them until you do again."

"Huh?"

Kokiri winked knowingly. "For your daughter. I'm sure she'll be a little handful, just like someone I know was." She laughed.

Kiki chose the biggest bell, polished it up, and wrapped it.

Then she was saying goodbye to Kokiri and Okino once again. This time there was none of the tension of her coming-of-age day.

"See you," her parents said, waving with a smile.

Kiki flew with Jiji straight for Koriko. As she glided, she could hear the bell ringing faintly in the bag hanging from her broom handle. It spurred her to fly even faster.

Before long, she could see the shining sea, and the town of Koriko appeared with its tall, box-shaped and triangular buildings.

"Look, it's our town!" Kiki shouted, and pointed.

Up ahead, the long shadow of the clock tower in the sinking evening sun stretched across Koriko, slicing it in half.

ABOUT THE AUTHOR

EIKO KADONO has published nearly two hundred original works and received many accolades, including but not limited to the Hans Christian Andersen Award and a place on the IBBY Honor List for *Kiki's Delivery Service*. She lives in the Kanagawa prefecture of Japan.